Crook's Hollow

Rob Parker

To Robin, the son I didn't think I'd be lucky enough to have.

Love you, kid.

And Becky, always.

Table of Contents

1

There was just the shallowest crescent of moon, high above. Everything else was black, and still.

The perfect night to get yourself killed, thought Thor Loxley.

'I know you might find it pathetic, but I think I'm going to beg for my life any minute now,' he said, just as a skull-jangling blow sent him down into the long grass. Wet tongues of green licked his face. He lay breathing heavily and caught sight of the disposable plastic overshoes on his assailant's feet.

'Decorator by trade? I have a feature wall I need repapering, if you're interested,' Thor said through ragged breaths, tensing as another fist ploughed his guts to tangled mush, sending him retching into the ground.

Thor was talking so much because he knew that if he didn't, his fear would rise and take over. He couldn't see anything of his adversary, it was far too dark; and whoever it was appeared to be dressed fully in black, even around the face.

Suddenly, he was pushed onto his front, his nose horribly close to his own fresh vomit, while a hand went fishing in his back pocket and pulled out his wallet.

'This is a robbery? That's it?' said Thor, but his assailant merely threw the wallet deeper into the field, lost instantly in the gloom. 'I don't get it,' Thor protested. 'What the fuck are you do—'

A backhand shot electricity through his jaw, shutting him up in an instant, putting him face down again, and he lay breathing shallowly, not sure if he was awake or not; everything inside and outside of him was equally dark

'You should have got on with it,' said the figure, in deep, aggressive tones that revealed that he was not only a man, but a man with very bad intentions indeed.

He must have been knocked out briefly, because he awoke with a start. The peace of the field was shattered by the growling bellow of an engine firing up, and Thor was flooded in light.

He struggled to see through the blinding glare, but could just make out the teeth of the thresher as they began to rotate, a wide bank of long knives spinning murderously. Then, just as suddenly, the whole rig started to crawl inexorably towards him. His panic surged and he watched in terror as a combine harvester bore down on him.

The teeth tore huge chunks out of the long grass just a few dozen feet in front of him, clawing it through its jaws into the pounding belly of the metal beast. He shuddered, thinking what this machine could do to a human body, what horrors it would make as it punctured and macerated the flesh and gristle, and struggled to rise but could not.

Through the whirling blades, as Thor lifted his head from the grass, he saw his assailant exit the cab of the combine and jump to the ground, leaving the machine lurching forward, evidently left in a low gear. 'You should have got on with it,' he shouted again as he ran into the inky night.

Panic wrung Thor tight. There was ten feet to go, and he could hear the knives whistling through the air. Move, he needed to move. Anything. Backwards. Get up. Go. Now.

2

He wouldn't go like this. He started scrabbling backwards, his legs feeling weak; it was like trying to run or hit someone in a dream—you try your hardest but you just can't do it.

In a weak gleam of moonlight, Thor recognised the missing letter on the front of the combine grille, just visible through the whirling teeth. He knew this machine. Knew it well. It was his father's, and Thor himself had used it in the past.

He scrambled on all fours like prey just ahead of the jaws of its hunter. He managed a few yards but the infernal machine kept pace with him.

With terror he felt his jeans snag and was yanked back as one of the twirling blades caught him, but as soon as he realised it had cut him through the denim, he was pulled forward by another force. Gravity. He hadn't seen it, but he was sliding down into a shallow ditch. He must be at one of the ends of the field, where the constant turning of machinery over the years had created a depression in the earth.

As he landed on his back, the blades spun just inches over his face and he was sprayed by fresh-cut greenery. Gears ground angrily as the blades buried themselves in the thick boundary hedge next to the depression, and the combine juddered, stuck. Still in gear, it fought to free itself. If the hedge gave way, and it sounded like it might, the wheels of the rig and the combine itself would soon drop down on top of him. He had seconds, no more.

He turned away from the roar of the combine and the groan of the hedge's roots, and began to crawl for his life, as unwanted thoughts clattered into his mind. What is it he should have 'got on' with? And why in hell was someone trying to kill him?

3

Thor got in around four in the morning. He was dripping wet and stank of mud and piss. He went straight into his dingy little bathroom and turned the hot taps on. He was stone cold sober now, the final dregs of the booze he had had last night long flushed away by adrenaline.

Nowt like attempted murder to get your head right after a night on the sauce, he thought; but in future, he'd stick with Alka-Seltzer, black pudding and paracetamol.

The steam in the room felt merciful on his skin as he peeled off the layers of nearly destroyed clothing. Flecks of shed mud rained down onto the curled lino. He checked himself over: aside from a few cursory scratches, some worse than others but no worse than if a cat had swiped at him, he had really got away with this one. The call had been close, the escape even closer. But here he was.

He had brought a bin bag in from the kitchen with him and, standing there starkers, stuffed all the clothes into it. He'd bin them later. He smelt himself, and scrunched his nose up. In the terror of the twirling knives, he had involuntarily gone number one. He had always thought he would have acted cool under extreme pressure, and he ended up doing the exact opposite.

The mystery of that hour loomed hard and heavy in the background, but his main thought was of how relieved and amazed he was to be alive. He lowered himself into the foamy water of the bath, shoving other thoughts back for a while.

It didn't take long for them to sweep back in.

Someone had just tried to kill him. There was no question of that.

Someone wanted him out of the picture.

But why? What possible thing could he, Thornton Loxley, of shittest name known to man, twenty-five years old, youngest brother of five much more accomplished siblings, and massively average in every way, have done to warrant being savagely attacked and left for dead?

He had no money—well, no real money. He had about four grand in his bank account, and double that figure in credit card debt. He worked on the bar in his local pub, The Traveller's Rest, and hadn't even done so much as pour a bad pint for one of the finicky locals. He had kept his head down most of his life, and couldn't imagine that he'd upset someone enough to make them want to kill him. He was a nobody, who had done nothing.

Well, he thought, as he pulled his head under the water, his short crew cut spreading the warmth quickly across his entire scalp, that had changed. Maybe he had done something serious. Maybe he had upset someone in a grand way. He must have.

And now that the door to such possibilities had creaked open, doubts snuck in and his mind raced. Now that he thought about it, maybe he did have a couple of ideas.

But he was sure that whoever had tried to kill him, hadn't seen that he'd survived—and that would give him the element of surprise. He'd find out who did this, and settle the score in some way. If that meant the police, it meant the police, but for the time being he would keep them out of it. No point flooding Crook's Hollow—the little village of three thousand souls that he had lived in all his life—with fluorescent jackets and door-knocking. All that ever does is make local people clam tight and stick to their own. Like him. He knew the community, and was sure he'd find out more by himself.

He decided to start first thing.

4

At seven sharp, he left his flat above the post office and made his way down the steep stairs at the back of the building, the rusted iron structure his only access to and from his front door. He didn't need to keep quiet; the landlords, Ahmed and Mo, would be opening up the post office about now. When the two brothers of Indian descent had bought the village post office, the purchase had caused a stir that Thor felt, even at fifteen. A decade later, the brothers were a big part of village life, loved by many and respected by most, and good friends to Thor.

The village of Crook's Hollow, named after a small valley secreted away in the fields on Crook's Farm, was the archetypal England village, both in scale and mindset. No more than a stopping point between bigger settlements on either side of it, it was a picture of bygone quaintness, from its simple street structure to its traditional architecture. Old brick framed by greenery. There were basic amenities, that's all. You could use your bank card in the post office, but that was made possible only a couple of years ago. The village hall was a decrepit, asbestos-insulated hovel housing a collection of old wooden chairs. The church, on the edge of the village, had lost most of its roof on nothing more than a blustery night a decade earlier, and the rector and his parishioners were still trying to fix it.

Over the years, a couple of housing developments had cropped up. An estate was built in the mid-sixties near the village school, and for a time in the decades either side of the millennium it became fashionable amongst what some would call the young and upwardly mobile. Others would call them yuppies. Of the village's three thousand residents, you were either a local or what the locals called a 'tourist,' but a village so small meant that the two groups brushed against each other every day, and the tourists had now started to outweigh the locals in both numbers and influence.

Thor himself was a local, and as he walked across the road from the post office in the direction of the estate, he pondered the state of the village he had lived in all his life. Everybody here knew everybody else's business, whether you liked it or not. For finding out why he was attacked last night, it was unnerving. On one hand, he was exposed— the Crook's Hollow grapevine was that short. On the other, someone would likely know something. The length of that grapevine again. He was confident he could get to the bottom of it.

The November morning was cool yet breezeless, and grey clouds hovered like smudged Zeppelins. Thor walked briskly, clad in thick boots, scuffed jeans, and a thick waterproof jacket—the same outfit he wore every day.

Dropping through the ginnel from the main road onto the estate, within five minutes he was at the house on Deadfern Road. Number 32, a house where he had spent many afternoons as a child after school, was a two-story detached affair with a single garage, small garden, and two-car driveway. It looked just like the one next to it, and the one next to that, and so on and so forth. It seemed that in the sixties there had been a dearth of architectural invention. Thor walked up the drive, noticing that all three cars were there, wedged into the smaller space like a game of automobile Tetris. They were all at home. During the night, he had come up with a few names, a few tentative lines of enquiry he wanted to check out, and this was the first and most likely on his list. He rang the bell, and knocked three times. Getting no answer, he knocked again. A couple of moments later, a white shape loomed in the frosted glass panel of the door, and the door swung open. A middle-aged woman wearing a once-fluffy, now off- white bathrobe, her dyed blonde hair mussed and her face so uncharacteristically shorn of thick make-up that he was taken aback at

how tiny her eyes really were, stood before him.

'Morning, Barb,' he said to the woman he had known since preschool. 'Sorry for the early wake up. Is Jason home?'

Barb looked both relieved and disappointed at the same time.

'Yes, Thornton, I'll get him,' she sighed, turning to the bottom of the stairs. 'Jason!' she bellowed.

'Thank you,' Thor said as Barb retreated up the stairs without a word. He heard her shout a second

24

time to her son, and then heard a deeper, muffled response. Thor walked back out to the driveway; he didn't want Jase's parents to hear what they were about to talk about. He waited while the morning birds trilled at the clouds, then heard the door opening.

The man who came down the steps was the same age as Thor, and looked like he'd lost a fight with both the Sandman and Jack Daniels.

'The fuck d'you want?' Jason said, while smoothing his bedhead.

Thor surveyed him closely, looking for a giveaway.

'Surprised to see me?' he asked, folding his arms across his chest, unconsciously puffing himself up to look more imposing.

'Well, you've got balls showing yourself at my house after last night,' said Jason, his voice a ragged croak.

'Yes, last night, let's talk about that.' 'You're no better than me, Thor.'

'Oh, I am. It takes a certain kind of shithouse to come after me like that.'

Thor could feel the rage rising in his chest, the anger at Jason's affront. 'Years we've been mates, Jase. Years. And you piss it all away because I was just doing my job, and you couldn't handle it.'

'You think I was in the pub last night because of you?'

'I'm not talking about the pub. I'm talking about afterwards.'

Jason knitted his brows. 'After the pub? What, you mean after you kicked me out in front of half the village?'

'You were doing coke off the disabled toilet seat, Jase. Pathetic. This is Crook's Hollow, not L.A.'

'There you go, up on your high horse again. The Hollow isn't as innocent as you think. You're in the minority, you know.'

Thor knew that Jason was right. Cocaine had seeped into the village and the neighbouring, flashier settlement of Windle Heath, starting with the younger sons and daughters of the wealthy in the early 2000s. Now even the housewives were at it, packing their septums in between school runs.

'You don't do it in the pub. If you can't go to your local pub without needing to line your nose with that garbage, it's a sorry fucking state of affairs isn't it?'

'Whatever.' Jason looked down, embarrassed to be admonished by his childhood friend. They had gone their separate ways as they'd matured, pursuing different things, and their relationship had been strained for a while.

'But dragging me out to the field... well, that's a new low. Even for a druggie scumbag like you.'

Thor was really fuming now, but Jason's expression was confused. 'After the pub? After the pub I went to Thompson's house. I was

nowhere near any fucking field.' 'Give over.'

'Fuck off if you don't believe me.' Jason took a step closer, and for the first time in their lives, the two men squared up to each other.

'You jumped me, assaulted me, and dragged me out to the field on the edge of the farm, just because I did the right thing,' said Thor, his chest pressed primally against Jason's.

'Watch the shit coming out of your mouth.'

The look in Jason's eye spoke volumes, his own hangover long since adrenalised with the buzz of accusation.

'You're saying you had nothing to do with it then?'

Thor was not a violent man, but since the previous night, something had clicked in him. A fail-safe had been activated, a preservation mode engaged; he was ready to defend himself if he had to.

'I don't know what you're on about. I'm saying that me and Thommo hung out in his living room, watching Storage Hunters and drinking knock-off ciders. Whatever you do on that bloody farm your family cares so much about is something I'm definitely not interested in. Your family have been lording it over everyone for years. Well, here's a tourist telling you to fuck off.'

Thor felt both furious and sad. He knew that people thought the Loxley family were on odd breed, with their deep roots and their wide grip on the land. It was one of the reasons Thor had distanced himself from his own blood; he didn't feel the same pull of the land and their place on it. He felt it was weird to be so obsessed with the past that it had such a daily impact on the present, so he had gravitated away.

But hearing these home truths from an old friend, and to hear those same words used in a way that would bury their old friendship once and for all, was a bitter pill for Thor to swallow, one that would stick fast on the way down.

'If I find out you lied to my face,' Thor said, backing away slightly but retaining eye contact, 'I'll be back here. And no amount of beak or booze will be able to numb what I'll do to you.'

Jason laughed. 'You always had a quick gob, but I've never seen you try to play hard before. I wouldn't recommend keeping it up.'

Head down, Thor walked back up the street to the ginnel to begin the walk back home.

5

Thor sat at his usual window table, pen in hand, mobile phone and coffee in front of him. A napkin with a few scrawled notes lay between his hands. The café was empty, in the usual fashion of Sunday mornings. Thor regularly stopped in Maud's Victorian Tea Shoppe for a cuppa, but never this early, and never on a Sunday. It only added to his disquiet.

His thoughts were preoccupied and dark, as he wrote down the names of anybody who may have had any kind of motive for attacking him the previous night. The first name down was Jason's, despite his assertions to the contrary, but he knew a quick fix way of clearing that up. On his mobile, he dialled Kev Thompson's house. He'd be able to back up Jason's story in a heartbeat. The phone was answered on its fifth ring.

'Mr. Popular,' answered Kev, in a voice that sounded decidedly more chipper than Jase's had earlier.

'I take it that means you and Jase did hang out last night?' Thor asked.

'Oh yes. Your antics came up. That and some cheap cider and

Storage Kings.'

Thor caught the error. 'He told me Storage Hunters.'

'Kings, hunters, pirates, magnates, it's all the same. Wheeler dealers trying to make garbage into gold. They all blend into one anyway.'

Something didn't fit. Not that he necessarily thought Kev was lying to him. All those crap shows were the same, mixing them up was hardly a smoking gun. But Kev was a tall guy and the guy who attacked him last night was pretty tall too… Could Jase and Kev have worked him over together?

'How tall are you, Kev?' 'Six four, why?'

'And you both were at your house last night from midnight onwards?'

'Yes. After you threw him out the pub, me and Jase did indeed commit the terrible crime of sitting at home, drinking cheap cider and watching trash TV. Happy?'

'Delighted.'

Thor hung up and wrote Kev Thompson's name on the napkin under Jason's name. In block capitals at the top of the napkin, he wrote, YOU SHOULD HAVE GOT ON WITH IT. Those words were driving him mad; he had no clue what they meant. But it was supposed to be the last message he'd ever hear.

He looked out of the window. Cars were heading in the direction of the church. The pull to Sunday-morning service was still strong in the village, even if a few of the middle-left pews had to be avoided, thanks to drips from the holes above.

Then an idea struck him. Church—that's why Maud's was empty.

And a plan hatched.

Whoever'd wanted him dead wouldn't know he'd lived. And if it was someone in the village, there was a fair chance they would be at the Sunday church service. And maybe, if he kicked up a bit of dust and worked out who wasn't best pleased to see him alive, he'd have a hope in hell of working out whatever it was he should have got on with in the first place.

Thor was realistic enough to know two things about himself—one, he could be an indignant sod if he put his mind to it. Just ask Jason, and the rest of his own family. And two? As much as he had his grievances with the way he'd been raised, there was one hangover from those times he still believed in. Problems get dealt with in house. No outsiders.

It was time to be a stubborn bugger and stick his nose in again.

6

Church itself, moreover what it embodied and not the pile of old bricks it had become, was never something that motivated Thor. He did, however, respect its position in the order of things in Crook's Hollow. Weekends came and went as sure as the rain, and just as sure was the fullness of the church on Sunday mornings. Thor had often wondered if adhering to such a routine was down to a genuine belief in the supposed Almighty, or simply that the decades-old rhythm of its tradition had become too ingrained to break.

The church—this church in particular—was a cornerstone and anchor point for many, and it contributed to so much in the community. Charity, fund-raising, knitting mornings, art classes, youth clubs, bowls tournaments—all encouraged by the church. For whatever reasons people went there, Thor saw its value.

Which made it all the more strange that this was the first time that Thor had been here in a year. Standing outside the old polished mahogany doors on this grey Sunday morning, he knew exactly why. They were over there, in the car park, clambering out of the old broccoli-green Land Rover Discovery they had had for years. His parents. And eventually, his siblings would appear too. A good old family reunion, he thought.

Their paths crossed regularly enough in the village, but there was something about the church that made a meeting uncomfortable. It was easy to be distant in the pub or the Sainsbury's in the next village along; it wasn't so easy to be so staid and unforgiving in the house of the Lord. Contrition and bridge-building would be expected—where better?

His mum and dad ambled through the graveyard next to the church, passing Agnes Loxley's grave and patting the headstone like always. A little reminder from son and daughter-in-law to old Ma Loxley, the long-departed matriarch: we are still here. Life still goes on.

Bunny Loxley caught sight of him first, and immediately tugged on her husband's sleeve. Thor found himself waving meekly, just as Wilkes Loxley VII made eye contact with him. The old man's eyes narrowed beneath his thick brow as if he were struggling to make sense of what he was seeing.

Bunny was a doughy woman with scraggly grey hair pulled back from her face in a bedraggled ponytail. She had never once worn a shred of makeup; her wide face showed every abundant wrinkle it possessed. She was dressed for church in a long wool coat that she had knitted herself back in the 1970s—same with the bag over her shoulder. Only the muddy Wellington boots were shop bought.

Wilkes Sr. was a man forged from softening concrete, wrapped in tweed. A behemoth in his earlier years, he now carried a slope in his shoulders that betrayed countless hours working the family farm. He wore a check shirt and a red wool tie. His hair was shoulder length, swept back from a face hard with stubborn angles. He looked like a Viking too proud to retire.

If Thor had thought about it earlier, he would have put them in these exact outfits. They dressed like this every Sunday, and had done for years.

Thor felt a vague longing, as if the bridge between the two parties was surely a lot smaller than he'd once thought, and that the events of the last couple of years could surely be swept away. But then he remembered the combine harvester—his own father's combine harvester—that had been used to try to kill him.

Thor wondered if the look his father was giving him at that moment was one of surprise—surprise at seeing his son alive. Would Wilkes Sr. try to arrange the death of his own son?

No time to think. They were upon him.

'Thornton,' his mother said in her paper-thin voice, reaching a hand up to his cheek. Thor looked at her and smiled meagerly. Despite everything, what kind of man shuns his seventy-year-old mother? 'It's very good to see you here.'

'I thought it was about time,' Thor lied. 'Wilkes.' His father put his hands in his pockets stiffly.

'To what do we owe the pleasure, Thornton? Still pissing away your legacy?'

Thor was ready for this.

'Just wanted to come to church. You've run me off from everywhere else, but this is one of those rare buildings in this village where your influence isn't the most important. Even though I expect the idea of playing God probably appeals to you.'

Wilkes iced over, the curls of his long grey hair rippling on his lapels. He looked at Thor with fire in his eyes. 'Watch your mouth. I won't tell you again.'

'Wilkes,' pleaded Bunny, putting an arm between the two men, separating them not for the first time. It saddened Thor, but he was too charged by the animosity coming off his father. Could this man really have tried to kill him? He decided to just go for it, just get the big question out there.

'You seem surprised to see me, Wilkes.' Thor tried but could not stare his father down, and the old man knew it.

'I'm always surprised to see you doing anything you are supposed

to.'

The words were like water off a duck's back to Thor. He had heard

39

it all before.

'Tell me about the old combine.'

'What? What the hell are you talking about?'

The confusion in his eyes and voice seemed real enough to Thor. 'The old combine. Big yellow thing with knives on the front. Where

is it now?'

Wilkes Sr.'s face was blank.

'I don't follow. Why do you want to know about the old harvester?

We replaced it, you know that.' 'Last night. Where were you?'

Now it was Bunny's turn to look lost. 'We were at home, Thornton.

What's going on?'

Thor suddenly realised that there were a few people gawping at them on the path, and he felt the burn on his cheeks. Those looks were everything he hated about this place, that voyeuristic hunger in quietly judging eyes.

'Nothing,' he said, cooling quickly. Nothing could be gained from having it out here and now, in full view of the community and its wagging tongues. Plus, there were other people to take in and consider. Bunny ushered Wilkes Sr. further down the path to the church entrance. His head was bowed in befuddled outrage. Thor would feel

bad, but the overall arrogance of the man had felt ever less forgivable.

7

Thor headed along the weed-choked rose beds, past the onlookers to the other door of the church, down near the altar, which was less often used. His plan was to sit near the front and turn to face everyone when the church was full, and in doing so reveal his survival. I'm still here, fuckers. Then watch for a giveaway—someone uncomfortable or surprised. Or failing that, something to jog his subconscious. He had barely seen his assailant, but maybe, in the fury of the attack, his mind had picked up one or two things about his attacker without his consciously realising it.

As the side door opened with a monstrous screech, he could see that any hopes of an unobtrusive entrance were dashed. The vicar was standing at the front, watching his amassing congregation, and turned to face Thor as he was blown in noisily by the breeze. Father Malkin couldn't help but look surprised. He had been the priest in Crook's Hollow for more than twenty years, and was familiar with the Loxley clan—and thanks to the look on his face, Thor felt sure that Bunny had bent his ear about her concerns for her youngest son. Thor gave a brief wave, and took a seat on the corner of the front pew.

Malkin came over immediately, walking with soft, measured steps, as if his connection to God was via the grace of his insoles. 'Thor,' he said, 'it's very nice to see you. Have you been keeping well?'

There was a twinkle in Malkin's eye that was either genuine concern or condescension. Thor couldn't tell which, but his paranoia took a little skip. Was this an eager cover? He dismissed it quickly, but it made him acknowledge awkwardly that the events of the previous evening had got him jumpy and quick to conclusions.

'I'm fine, thanks, Father. I just remembered it had been a while since I had been here, and I thought today was as good a day as any.'

'Are you sure you're alright?' Malkin asked in a lower voice, as if he were somehow sensitive to Thor's last few hours.

'How do you mean?' Thor's gut tightened.

'Your face looks sore,' said the priest with concern.

Thor had completely forgotten. In fact, he had got straight up and dressed that morning, and couldn't even remember looking in the mirror. He was sore as all hell, yes, but his adrenaline and desire to get to the bottom of things had masked it. He must be inkblotting good and purple across parts of his face by now. Maude hadn't mentioned in the cafe, but then she had always been a private lady. That couldn't account for his mother not mentioning it though, never mind his father. Hurt welled in Thor, and not just in his face.

'I'm fine, Father. Just a bit of a fall.'

'As long as you're sure, Thor. If you need an ear, I'm here.'

A hush had descended as the last stragglers entered the church and sat down. Father Malkin moved to the front, and Thor took his opportunity. He stood and slowly removed his coat before turning around to survey the congregation.

I'm still here, fuckers. So, who wanted me dead?

Many sets of eyes fell on him, appraising him. Some were the blank stares of people he didn't know, some were the curious stares of people he knew to a degree, and some were the harder gazes of people he knew very well.

He took an inventory of the faces before him.

His parents' eyes were fixed on him, Wilkes Sr. with his jaw set obtusely, utterly resolute in his disapproval. Bunny looked at him with an air of sad acceptance, her face pretty much asking the question of what had become of her son while simultaneously answering it with disappointment.

He could see Barb Dwyer, Jason's mum, her own eyes now made up back to their normal size. He could see all his siblings and they were all looking at him. He had never felt so aware of himself and his failings as their gazes landed upon him.

Wilkes Loxley VIII, the eldest Loxley son, now forty and balding but with his father's indignant brow and jaw, and somehow an even redder face. His wife Theresa sat next to him, their two preteen boys either side of her.

On the row in front of her was Mercy Loxley, late thirties, eldest sister and perennial spinster. Her hair was a birds-nest tangle the colour and texture of straw. She was not for marrying and anyone who cared to listen knew it. She sat next to Crewe, Thor's next brother, who in turn sat next to Hollis, a year younger than Crewe. They looked alike except for the fact that Crewe wore a long beard; Hollis had tried to match it but couldn't, and sported a dangling scruff of wispy strands.

The three of them were unmarried, but that chain was broken by Rue Turner, née Loxley, who, at thirty-three, was the second youngest before Thor. She sat with a baby in her arms, three blond girls aged four to seven along the row next to her and her husband Barry on the end. He was a big, burly man, not a farmer but still a man of the outdoors and manual labour. As a road worker, he worked all hours God sent him (apart from the ones God set aside for worship, of course) on the never-ending roadworks on the nearby M6, M62, and M56 motorways, all of which helixed themselves inside out in a series of junctions a few miles outside of Crook's Hollow. With six mouths to feed, including his own, it was no wonder he was a workaholic and today, as always, he looked exhausted and hungover.

Looking at them like this, he felt more and more like the outcast, the black sheep. He was an accident, he knew that. After Rue, they were not expecting to have another child, but eight years and one botched vasectomy later, Thor came along.

He caught sight of his boss, Martin Campbell, who threw Thor a confused glance, presumably in response to his injuries. He wore a neat side-parting, wind-fluffed at the back where he hadn't smoothed it down, and had never been seen without an ironed button-down shirt, today with a Sunday tie. Campbell had served pints to Thor since the day Thor was able to buy them, and more than a few times before. He had always been a straight shooter with Thor, and a fair employer.

Thor felt as if he could stand no longer, as more eyes turned to him, and he sat down. The service started, and Thor quickly buried himself in his own thoughts.

The glares he had received from his own family were a mix of pity, disdain, apparent sadness and obvious contempt. He had let them all down, according to their own code of values, but was it enough to kill him? Their own blood? It was a thought that never left him for the duration of the service, and the more time that went by, the more he began to fear the worst.

8

Thor left the church before the last 'Amen' had finished echoing in the broken rafters, more confused than ever and definitely in no mood to be confronted by his kin. He wanted relief and a sympathetic ear, and that would only come from his darling Roisin.

He high-tailed through the graveyard under the darkening sky, patted Ma Loxley without breaking stride, and hopped straight into his decrepit Astra. The key didn't work, and never had during his time of ownership, but it was such a rusted shit-tip that he never locked it anyway. When he was out of the car park and on the safety of the road, he fumbled his headphones into his ears and called Roisin.

She answered after four or five rings, and he pictured her stretching her way languidly out of a lie in. He imagined her in her pyjamas, in the tiny bedroom of her caravan, and hoped she would still be in bed by the time he got there. His Roisin: his one-time guilty pleasure, now fast approaching something so much more.

'Good morning, stranger,' she purred, evidently having caught his name on caller ID.

'You still in bed?' Thor asked. 'If not, please get back in it.'

She laughed with an uninhibited throatiness that was both unbecoming and sexy.

'Yes, I'm still here,' she said. 'You coming up?'
'Definitely.'

'Well, I've seen that the family is up and at 'em down by the main gate. You OK with that?'

'I'll slip in the back way. Not all that up for a telling-off this morning.'

Their relationship, even at this early stage, was a peculiar one. As few people as Thor could manage actually knew about it. Thor would usually be up for the scrap and the argument, but... not today. He just wanted to see her.

'I'll crack the window, just hop in.' 'I'll be there in five.'

'I'm going nowhere. You'll know where to find me.'

Thor smiled at the very thought, but caught sight of himself in the rearview mirror. It was the first time he had seen his face since the assault, and no amount of low bedroom lighting could hide how black and blue he was.

'Listen, Roisin, when you see me… don't worry, but my face is a bit of a mess.' The line went quiet.

'Are you OK? Should I be worried?' Roisin asked, her voice brittle as an eggshell.

'No, I'm fine. But if you have any ice handy, that'd be decent.'

9

After parking in a muddy side road, in the shade of a stand of moss- clad silver birch, Thor checked that the only living things that had

caught sight of him were the ragtag herd of sheep below. Satisfied, he made his way down the shallow slope to join them in Crook's

Hollow—not the village, but the actual Crook's Hollow, the valley on

the Crooks' land after which the entire village was named.

The Hollow itself was a lazy shallow V etched into the green, as if dug by a gigantic, chubby finger, which flooded easily in even the lightest showers. A drystone wall ambled around the eastern ridge, while the rest of the valley floor was merely grass and little else. It was pretty and iconic in the most British of ways. As Thor walked, picking his way through the mounds of fresh droppings and mole hills, he saw Roisin's trailer up tight next to the wall, its rear looking over the Hollow, its front facing the open fields down to Crook's Farm. It was a nice spot, and one that Thor was getting more accustomed to spending time at.

As a Loxley the Hollow was off limits, but his ostracisation from his own family had seen a relaxing of the convention. He would never be a Crook, but he was barely a Loxley now either. The Crooks were the Loxleys' natural enemies, a clan rivalry cast in stone generations prior to the contemporary tendency to forgive and forget old quarrels. Still, Thor couldn't help thinking of the long-dead brethren of both clans spinning in their graves at the thought of a Loxley and a Crook about to have sex. In fact, Thor thought with a smile, their horror at such inter-clan coitus may be the only thing that the two families would ever have agreed on.

To Thor's eye, the trailer could either have been cream or a mucky off-white, as he walked beneath it on the brow. He took the steeper ascent to the stone wall, keeping the caravan firmly between himself and possible eyes. Having scaled the wall, he inched along to the high window of the bathroom, which was cracked open, just as Roisin promised. He perched his backside on the ledge, shucked out of his boots and clattered them together to beat the mud and shit off them, before going in.

He was immediately swallowed by a warm steam cloud, lost in a sudden haze.

The bathroom was tiny and it didn't take him long to see that he wasn't alone. In the shower cubicle to the right of the window stood Roisin, naked and dripping. The look in her eyes made Thor's knees quake. Her black hair was streaked back from her forehead and down over her shoulders, and her face was composed of big sovereign-gold eyes, over an elegant nose and full lips. In the steam, he could make out little else but the most inviting of shapes.

'I know I said I'd be in bed, but I thought you wouldn't mind this little plot twist,' she said. Her concern was there, but masked, and she was just about pulling it off. Before she could finish saying 'Poor baby, what happened to you?' Thor was in and upon her, saving the answers for when their blood wasn't pounding so fiercely.

Sometime later, they lay in the narrow bed in the bedroom, Thor staring at the peeling floral cladding above, while Roisin traced the bruises on his face with a bag of frozen Alphabet-Bites she had fetched from the kitchenette. He had just told her everything and left nothing out.

'You should have got on with it...' Roisin said, leaving the words

hanging in the air over their heads like mistletoe.

Thor glanced at her out of the corner of his eye, watching her jaw and bottom lip jut out in thought. Her brow was wrinkled in concern, and she looked at him earnestly. It was the tiny moments like these, when she was at her least self-conscious and at her most honest and naked (not literally, even though she was and he liked that too) he could feel the hole in himself widening to allow her in deeper, the hole he himself was digging for her, into which he was falling too. His love for her was growing, regardless of scandal.

The people that Thor and Roisin were, and the kin that they had descended from—farming people, prone to action—dictated that they found themselves speaking of solutions as opposed to their fears. Thor's grandfather, one of the many other Wilkes' of yesteryear, once told him, 'Taters don't grow better with frettin', only your hands can help.' It was about the most profound thing he'd ever said.

'Who might say such a thing to you?' she asked, bringing the thawing bag to a nasty red welt on his ribs.

'Who might say such a thing to anyone?' Thor replied. 'It implies I'm late with something. So what am I late with?'

'Rent?'

'That would be the obvious one, given it's probably my only real financial obligation. But no, I'm all up to date there. Besides Mo and Ahmed are cool, they'd just have a quiet word with me if something was amiss. And besides, who would murder someone over late rent?'

'Library books all returned on time?'

'I don't think mowing people down with farm machinery has started replacing fines for late books. Besides, I haven't set foot in the library since they stopped stocking comics.'

'Mistaken identity?'

'Nope, I don't think so. He checked my ID, remember, before tossing it back out into the field.'

'The field… Maybe he left something out there about himself by accident. A clue. Evidence. Maybe we should go back there and have a look?'

'That's a good idea.'

He pulled her body tighter to his. Despite the uncertainty of the moment he felt a bright safety and warmth in her presence, amplified by being so close to her. She squeezed back, her care and worry evident in the strength of her grip.

'Not bad for a dirty Crook,' he said.

She was about to protest the jibe when their solitude was shattered by two pounding knocks on the caravan door.

10

Roisin answered the door, having pulled on a jumper and jeans in record time, while Thor waited in the bedroom. As the cold air hit her face, she saw two men she immediately recognised, a feat seemingly made all the easier by the fact that they were identical.

'G'morning,' said Wendell Crook laconically, standing side by side with his brother Ward. 'Mum's looking for you.'

'Morning, Wendell,' Roisin replied. She had her own issues with her family, issues that had seen her banished to the far reaches of their property in an old caravan. 'Did it really need both of you to come out here for that? You could've sent me a text. Or better yet, Mum could have.'

Wendell smiled thinly, causing his thick red moustache to stretch on his lip like a tired caterpillar. Ward, unhelpfully wearing his facial hair exactly the same way, mirrored the gesture and for a moment it looked to Roisin like the two caterpillars were locked in a mating ritual of imitation. 'We know he's here,' said Wendell.

Roisin didn't act one bit surprised—or intimidated. 'So you thought you'd come and protect me? Twin knights in shining armour.'

'He shouldn't be here, you know.' Wendell's smile darkened. 'This here is my caravan. I can have over who I like, when I like.'

'The land.' Wendell grew more serious with each word. 'He shouldn't be on this land. His family have had enough to do with our land, no Loxley should be anywhere near it.'

'Oh, that old chestnut.' Roisin smiled and turned to Ward. 'Are you going to say anything, or are you just the hired muscle?'

'What he said,' muttered Ward.

Despite the two being physically identical, the brothers couldn't have been more different. Now in their early forties, they still were lucky enough to have thick red hair, eyes of Everest blue, and both were built like tree stumps. In terms of personality, they were wildly different, and Roisin knew from experience that her dig at Ward being the hired muscle was more than a little true. Where Wendell was gobby, in-your-face, and mischievous, Ward was dark, reticent, and mean.

'So you've come to escort him off the property, is that it?' asked Roisin.

Ward's eyes betrayed a fleeting excitement at the mere thought. 'Nothing so dramatic,' answered Wendell before raising his voice

to shout into the trailer. 'Just want him to know we are here and keeping an eye on him.'

In the bedroom, Thor had just finished pulling his socks up when he heard the invitation. He had actually listened to the entire conversation and had, up to now, been happy to keep a low profile. The animosity towards him, so pointless in the grand scheme of things, irked him and another thought entered his head: Could they be so protective of Roisin as to want him dead? Did the Loxley name really boil their blood that much?

The pieces began to slot all too quickly in Thor's mind and before he knew it he was on his way to confront the brothers. By the time he had got to the door he had reasoned, even though he only saw one, that two men could easily have been there last night, one to attack him and one to start the combine engine. When he appeared next to Roisin at the door, he was fizzing inside.

'Fellas, I've been doing my best to go under the radar, and when I've not managed that I've at least tried to be courteous. But hunting me down and railroading me off the property is hardly going to promote progress, is it?'

'Always the same,' said Ward. 'Bait the mouth of the rat's nest, and eventually he'll stick his head out.' His tone dripped with aggressive, almost perverse sarcasm.

'That's not helping,' retorted Thor, stepping down off the steps. 'Anything you want to tell me about? Wait, I've got to take your mental dexterity into account. Last night: where were you?'

'Watch your face-hole,' Wendell warned.

'Yeah, yeah, I've been told that like four times already today. First time with face-hole, though. Answer the question.'

There was a moment of silence as the three men examined each other, and it became apparent to Thor that the longer the wordless moment persisted, no alibi was being offered.

'Your silence is pretty deafening, gents. What's on your mind?' Thor pressed his advantage, looking them in the eye and keeping a close grip on his cool. But he could feel his anger rising, hot with volcanic unpredictability.

Ward broke the moment with an icy smirk. 'Loxley prick,' he seethed. 'All the same, aren't you... All high and mighty, even when you bite off more than you can chew.'

'You're not doing much to put my mind at ease, Ward. Again, what were you up to last night?'

'Something that'll piss your dad right off,' Wendell spat. Ward looked at him immediately with a questioning glance.

That was a curve ball for Thor. His dad? What would upset his dad? To Thor's mind, the idea of him getting hurt would likely not upset Wilkes Sr. An unexpected wash of protective feeling rolled over Thor at the mention of his father's well-being, and the heat of the moment took over. Thor marched straight up to Wendell, but before he got within two feet of him, Ward had him in his grasp.

Thor cursed himself for acting so foolishly, and he struggled as Ward slipped him into some kind of choke hold. Thor had never been in a choke before and a strange detached slice of him marveled at it. His hearing went muffled, like he was in forty feet of water, and sparks frittered at the edges of his vision like moths on fire. He could hear Roisin pleading with Ward to let him go, and his legs turned into gummy bears stuffed down his jeans. The moths got bigger and darker, and his knees buckled. He could hear laughter louder than Roisin's voice, and it took all his concentration to work out that it was Ward laughing in his ear. He slipped from consciousness.

The last words he heard, while the moths blocked out all else, was Wendell's bellow: 'He started it, and his family before him. He should've got on with it…'

11

Thor came round to find Roisin standing over him. Half his face felt slick and cool, yet somehow gritty, and he realised it was the muddy puddle he had been dumped in.

'There he is. Welcome back,' said Roisin, kneeling by his side stroking his cheek. 'I'm really sorry about that. Just take a minute there. I've seen him do that so many times—it's like his party piece. One Christmas he did it on Cassie.'

'Cassie?' Thor croaked, while trying to right himself.

'Our last sheepdog. And that was only because Grandpa had already fallen asleep after too much sherry with pudding.'

Weird family, thought Thor, as he sat up straight. He was feeling better by the second, his faculties stronger with each breath. In some strange way he felt a pang of respect for Ward, in amongst the distaste.

Now there's a man who doesn't hesitate. Thor felt he could learn from that going forward.

You should have got on with it. The very words from last night. That couldn't be a coincidence. And to pursue it further, he'd need some tangible proof they were involved.

He was fairly sure where he could start looking for some, so he pulled himself to his feet. 'No rest for the wicked. You mind driving to the field off Mill Lane?'

'Of course not,' said Roisin, reaching inside the caravan door for her keys on the kitchenette counter. She closed the door behind her and started off down the track. Thor loved that she had only just shrugged on whatever clothes she had to hand, and was ready to roll without a moments glance in the mirror - not that she needed it. Ready for anything, his gal.

'Your door—don't lock it?' Thor asked, stumbling after her.

'I'd have thought you'd worked out that with Ward and Wendell around, security isn't that high a priority here.'

'No, I suppose not.'

Roisin's rust-flecked Vauxhall Corsa sat by the gate where the drystone wall cut away from the Hollow and across the field. A single- track road leaked in a straight arrow down to a series of farm buildings a quarter of a mile away—the main body of Crook's Farm.

Thor opened the five-bar gate while Roisin got the Corsa going. A couple of tries and it was away, and as soon as the engine caught, a gaudy pop song filled the quiet morning air at obscene volume. Thor smiled. That was Roisin, through and through. Happy in her own little world, doing her own thing.

He hopped into the car and hunkered down in the seat. Roisin took the car a bit too fast for the battered track, but before long they emerged into the smoother roads of the farmyard, and Thor kept his head down as they swung through. From his position below the window line, he could see Roisin waving at a few people as she gunned through. Thor couldn't tell if she was waving to farmhands or family members, but either way he was glad to progress unseen. Everyone loved gossip, and in a place like Crook's Hollow, gossip was like currency, passed furtively in shadows and across bright dining tables with the same glee.

They passed into the shadows of the main barns, and Thor realised Roisin had taken the route farthest from the main house. Good, thought Thor. The farmyard itself soon passed and she was out between some beech hedges onto the public road. It was only then that Thor straightened in his seat.

'Safe to come out?' he asked.

'Yep. Only a few of the boys kicking about today,' she replied.

'I bet they love you—the beautiful farmer's daughter they catch a glimpse of from time to time.'

'Worked on you, didn't it?' she replied with a smile.

Thor couldn't help but smile back, because she was so right. He had seen her many times and felt for all sorts of reasons—from simply the gulf between the families right through to the fact that he felt a girl of Roisin's beauty was clearly out of his league—that he would never have a chance with her. Fate clearly had other ideas.

The sun was shining, even though the air had a crispness to it. It felt a bit strange—a meteorological paradox.

'Do you buy into it? The talk of the floods, I mean,' he asked, his mind wandering. Recent news bulletins had torrential rain in the coming days, with some of the more paranoid outlets using the dreaded word floods, but any such time felt a world away from this pleasant winter morning. It had been an unseasonably warm autumn, and winter hadn't even looked a remote possibility until very recently.

'I reckon there'll be rain, yeah,' Roisin replied. 'Not sure we are going to be surfing out of here, but it'll probably get a bit wet.'

Thor didn't know of any time when there had been a flood here in Crook's Hollow. The idea just seemed inconceivable, like a meteor strike or an alien landing. So, to himself and most others he knew of, it was mostly dismissed.

Three minutes more driving, while another pop song came on which Roisin knew all the words to, even though Thor thought it was very generous to call it a song, or even music, for that matter, and they were there, parking alongside the road next to a thick brambled hedge overhung with sycamores.

The road was utterly quiet, save for the simmer of leaves in the trees above and the odd chirrup of unseen birds. Thor got out and started towards the field's entrance, a creaking stile used primarily by dog walkers. Roisin slipped her hand into his as they walked, as if tuned in to his nerves and offering him reassurance.

They hopped the stile and looked at the field ahead of them. It was fairly sizeable, about ten hectares to Thor's eyes, but was left fallow. The grass was long and patchy, undulating softly in a rolling rustle. On the far side, the bottoms of its huge wheels hidden by the climbing grass, stood the combine, just where it had stopped the night before when Thor freed himself. Its jaws were still clamped tight in the hedge, which had been pushed back awkwardly.

Roisin's grip tightened and her pace slowed. They started walking towards the combine, their swishing footsteps the only sound. Once there, the scene of the struggle was visible, and Roisin gasped and covered her mouth.

The grass was matted down in patches. Dark flecks of blood spattered the grass.

'Oh my God,' whispered Roisin, as she turned to embrace Thor, the gravity of what had happened to him painted starkly in the light of day.

'Now you know why I look like this,' Thor whispered back. 'Who could have done this to you…'

'Some nasty bugger or other,' said Thor, as he smoothed her hair. 'I'm alright, you know.'

'I know,' she said, and their eyes met again. It led to a quick urgent kiss, and Thor had never felt more connected, nor more loved than in that moment.

'Let's see what we can find.'

They walked hand in hand around the site, before Roisin stopped in her tracks.

'Wait,' she said. 'Aren't we supposed to leave it untouched? For the police? Won't we mess up any evidence?'

'I'm not going to the police yet,' Thor replied. 'Whoever did this should believe I'm dead, that is, if they haven't seen me already this morning. I was after the element of surprise.'

Roisin suddenly left his grip and walked to the edge of the flattened grass. 'I see something.' She bent down.

'My wallet,' said Thor. 'Great.'

'At least you'll get your money back.'

'All seven quid of it. Bank card and ID is here, though, so that saves me a job of cancelling them.'

'But why? Why take out your wallet and chuck it aside? Seems so stupid,' said Roisin.

Thor turned back to the combine, flexing his wallet in his hands, bending the old leather. At last something made sense to him.

'It was to ID my body. That combine was supposed to scramble me to jam. Whoever did this wanted to make sure my body could be identified. They'd find my body, search the field, find the ID. It'd look like one big accident.'

'Jesus.'

'They wanted me dead, and they wanted everyone to know I was dead too.'

'But for God's sake why?' 'I don't know.'

Thor glanced around the field—then he felt something. A prickle of instinct, a nag of memory.

Something close yet shrouded. Something else making sense.

The field. Where they stood. What was it about this place?

His eyes suddenly caught a glint in the green by the combine cab. He picked it up immediately. It was a thin, clear tube with a black sort of cap adapter at one end—a vial of some kind.

'A vaporiser cartridge,' said Roisin.

'Finally something to go on.' He rolled it over in his hand. It was empty, and he gave it a sniff. 'Smells like bleach and blueberries.'

'You can buy flavoured ones these days.' 'So... our killer vapes. Narrows it down a bit.'

Thor started running through the suspects in his mind. He knew very few vaporiser users, which certainly drew the net tighter, and one name from his original list came to mind instantly: his old school mate, Jason Dwyer.

Dwyer was always vaping in the pub, because you were allowed to. No EU directive had stopped vaporisers from being used in public places.

Suddenly, he had it. The field! How could he have been so dense? He just never came here, never bothered to think about such things since he'd left Loxley Farm. It was—

'Thor, look.' Thor saw Roisin pointing back to the field entrance.

Three figures were walking towards them.

'Who the hell is that?' he mused. Roisin came to him. He spoke quietly. 'Don't say anything about last night.'

She nodded back firmly. Thor felt like it was them against the world—a grimy northern Bonnie and Clyde.

As the three people closed in, Thor saw they were two men and one woman, dressed all rather well in suit and tie and a trouser suit, respectively. They all appeared to be middle-aged, and could have been three siblings thanks to their similar appearance.

'Hi there,' said one of the men. He had grey hair with stubborn gold streaks in it slicked back from his brow, and crisp stubble dusted his chin like specks of tinfoil. His voice exuded confidence and an accent that, even though Thor couldn't place it, was unmistakably not from round these parts.

'Hey up,' said Thor, holding his position and giving nothing away. 'Nice day for a walk before the weather comes in,' said the man.

His sidekicks wore smiles of the purest smugness. 'If you believe everything the papers tell you.'

'Good man. Good man.' There was a gleeful edge to the man's reaction, as if he enjoyed Thor's. 'I'm Lionel Clyne.'

'Good morning, Lionel,' Thor replied steadily, holding firm. 'Can I make a wild guess at who you two are?'

This was getting too strange. First the attempt on his life, and now guessing games with a besuited weirdo at the site of the attempted murder. It was one veer too far into X-Files territory. Taking Roisin's hand, he started to walk away from the newcomers.

'It's Thornton Loxley and Roisin Crook, isn't it?' Clyne said, rooting Thor and Roisin to the spot.

'Quite the story, aren't you?' Clyne continued. 'Not that I don't like it. I love it. Love against the odds, following your gut and all that, tremendous. Very Romeo and Juliet.'

Thor was baffled. How did this guy know?

'Romeo and Juliet was a love affair between a couple of kids that resulted in murder and suicide,' Roisin said. 'I hardly think that fits.'

'Fair point, Miss Crook. Forbidden love was what I was alluding too, but there you go.' He looked past the pair of them at the combine. 'Well, that's seen better days.'

'Is there a reason you're here, Mr. Clyne?' said Thor. He was fed up being jerked around by people. He wanted answers—no more guessing.

'Just getting the lay of the land, really. Getting a sense of the scale of things here. It's lovely, isn't it?'

'Who are you, Clyne, and what do you want?' Thor said.

'Me? I'm just a simple engineer,' Clyne replied with a shark's smile. 'And a fan of bright young things going places.'

'Is there a reason you talk in riddles, or is it a syndrome of some kind?'

'You are lively, I'll give you that.'

'And you're boring me to tears—I'll give you that. Let's go Roisin.' 'The village hall, behind the church,' Clyne said. 'There's an event

there this afternoon, at two o'clock. Would be great if you could attend—both of you.'

'You're having a bake sale, how nice.'

Thor marched straight past him. As he and Roisin walked, he could just make out Clyne's laughter.

'I like him!' said Clyne in the distance.

'What was that all about?' asked Roisin, who was keeping pace at his side.

'I honestly don't know, sweetheart, and I'm not sure I want to find out either.'

A black Range Rover was parked right behind Roisin's Corsa. It had tinted windows, a current plate and black rims.

'Simple engineer, my arse,' said Thor.

'We could do with finding out who he is. What do you think about the event at two? Want to go? I have to admit, it's got me interested.'

'I'm not sure,' replied Thor. He looked back down the road, a road he had travelled up and down every day of his youth, going to school and back, or going into the village to go to the shops. It was very near home. His old home. 'There's something I need to check up on. Can I give you a call in a bit?'

'Sure. Are you OK?'

'Yeah, I just… I need to go and see my family. And I'm not sure it'll go down too well.'

'Well I'd love to meet your folks properly, but I'm not sure today is

the best time. I think I've got a bike helmet in my boot if you want it for a bit of extra protection.'

Thor gave her a sideways glance and a smile, but he was at least partly tempted to take her up on it

12

Thor made the short walk in about five minutes, and it had only taken that long to decide that he was going nowhere near his parents. He was still going back to Loxley Farm, but there was another family member he needed to see.

The lane soon grew less leafy and more flat, and the bulk of the Loxley Farm buildings loomed like an old factory on the horizon. The barns were just as he remembered them, the roads still just as battered and potholed. There was no gate as such, no official entrance, just a gap in the wire fencing, which he passed through with speed. If he were to take a right, he would pass through the barns and end up at the weathered two-story frontage of Loxley farmhouse, home to his mother, father, the three middle elder siblings, and their various cats and dogs.

He instead took the left, walking along the dirt track to the grain storage tanks, which looked more like missile silos. Pressed right up to the tanks sat a bungalow, whose front lawn was like a seabed festooned with the shipwrecks of kids' bikes and toys—Rue and Barry's place.

When Rue and Barry got married, and then had kids, Thor's parents had undertaken to look after them the only way they knew how: by smothering them with Loxley rites and traditions, suffocating them with the thick smog of family. Which meant, among other things, building a bungalow for them on an obscure corner of the property, so that they would never escape. The bungalow was a short, squat development frosted in sky-blue paint and perennially unfinished. It had been started ten years ago, built by Wilkes Sr. and his other sons (Thor included, as a fifteen-year-old) but Rue's first pregnancy ended sooner than the build did, and a brief pause in construction to greet the birth of their first born had somehow gone on until the present day. There were still piles of bricks stacked under the front windows, originally meant for a utility room of some kind. One day.

As Thor opened the small picket fence gate, two dogs appeared from round the back of the house in a frantic burst of fur and teeth.

'Easy!' he shouted on reflex, hoping the dogs remembered him. They did. Otter was a muddy brown mongrel terrier with a healthy dollop of greyhound heaved in at some stage way back. Beaver was second, a bulldog with a jaunty canter and a big smile. They ran around Thor's shins with glee, and he patted them with simple joy.

'Nice to see you, boys,' he said, as he walked to the house. The door opened almost immediately and his sister Rue emerged, baby glued to hip. She wore a faded denim shirt over thick patterned tights, and boots. Her blonde hair was pulled back from her face, and she looked youthful, but also exhausted. That's what four young kids will do to you, thought Thor. He smiled on seeing her.

'Hi, sis,' he said.

Rue looked at him with pursed lips. The baby also seemed apprehensive. Finally she sighed.

'If you looked bad at a distance, I should have guessed you'd look worse up close. What in God's name happened to you?' She surveyed his face with concern.

Thor reached for the baby, adopting a daft grin to soothe the wary infant. The baby went to him without fuss, and immediately grabbed his bottom lip. 'Hello, Andrew. At last, someone in this family with a sensible name. The kids still at Sunday school?'

Rue playfully tagged him on the arm. 'Yeah, I don't know what I'll do when they eventually get bored of it. The quiet on Sunday lunchtimes is the highlight of my weekend.'

Barry appeared in the doorway behind Rue wearing a high- visibility jacket. The creases in his tired face suddenly cleared when he caught sight of Thor's face.

'Jesus, Thor, what the hell happened to you?' he said, before rummaging behind the door.

'You know I'm a clumsy bugger at the best of times,' Thor answered.

Barry pulled out a pair of scarred work boots, and stamped them on. 'Well, be careful, you daft eejit.'

Barry always seemed to know what side his bread was buttered on, and Thor's arrival provoked the spectre of impending family politics, none of which he wanted any part of. He said goodbye to Rue and the baby, nodded to Thor, then left.

They went inside. The house was just as Thor remembered it: cramped, lived in, with a faint pervasive odour of agriculture, as if more of the active farm just yards away leaked in with every opening of the front door. But this was Rue's place, and thanks to his sister he had enjoyed many times here and had always felt comfortable and welcome.

When Thor was born, there was such a gap in the ages of the siblings that the eldest, aged fifteen and fourteen at the time, saw him as some kind of strange pet who had appeared too late in the day to be truly interesting or useful. All except for Rue, who was seven, and loved her baby brother. She had a maternal streak already fully developed by dolls and farm animals, and she was magnetised to Thor. Consequently, with the clamour and demands of all the older siblings, Rue had taken care of Thor for much of his formative years.

They went into the kitchen, which was as faded as an old Polaroid. Remnants of their breakfast still sat on the table, and Rue checked the teapot briefly. Satisfied, she put the kettle on.

'I'm sorry I've not been around in a while,' said Thor while taking a seat at the table, placing Andrew onto his knee carefully. He loved kids, and thanks to the number Rue had had, he got quite a bit of practice with them.

'I'm not surprised,' said Rue, taking a seat opposite him, absentmindedly brushing crumbs into her hand. It seemed as if she couldn't switch off at all.

'Well, I'm sorry either way.'

'It's alright, Thor, you're a big boy now, you can look after yourself.' 'I've not been able to talk to the others about it,' Thor said, nodding

in the general direction of the farm, and his other siblings.

'You've not even talked to me about it.' Rue took the handful of crumbs and dropped them in the huge plastic bin in the corner of the room. She then picked up the boiled kettle and made the tea. 'How long ago was it now?'

'Two years, almost,' said Thor, without missing a beat. It was about to get uncomfortable.

Abruptly, two years back, Thor had had a huge disagreement with his father, which had resulted in Thor packing his bag and leaving the property. Mo and Ahmed at the post office had offered him the flat upstairs at a reduced rate until he found his feet, which he quickly did. Since then, those same feet had not once set foot on the old farm he had called home all his life. It hurt at first, but now it was nothing more than the way things had to be. Thor was stubborn, as was Wilkes Sr. There would be no budge from either.

'Obviously we got Dad's side of things,' said Rue.

'I can guess that was the only part that our brothers and sisters were interested in,' Thor answered.

'I can't speak for them, but the general perception was that you didn't want to be a Loxley anymore.'

That seemed to prod Thor in the ribs, the sense of injustice. His choices and thoughts had been pre-decided without his voice, but then he remembered that that was the whole problem in the first place. He hated that his decisions had been taken from him. He felt he was from a different generation, and a different way of thinking, and when Wilkes Sr. worked that out, it had been too late.

'Can I trust you with something?' said Thor.

'Of course you can,' replied Rue. She was guarded, seemingly mindful that it must demand a degree of effort for Thor to reach out like this.

'I don't want anyone to find out, because there's a list of people I trust at the minute and it's not very long.'

'I better be on that list.' Rue smiled and placed her hand on the table in front of her brother. It wasn't a touch, but it would do for now, Thor thought.

'Someone tried to kill me last night, with the old combine harvester.'

Rue's eyes widened instantly as if Thor's words were a shot of adrenaline. She looked down at the floor, and then immediately back up to him. 'Jesus,' she whispered, before catching her language and crossing herself hastily. 'Here? In the Hollow?'

'Yes. Somewhere that, the more I think about it, the more important it could be.'

'How did it happen? Did you see who did it?' Rue asked, as she took his hand. She squeezed hard, and

Thor squeezed back. He had missed his sister terribly, and he had enjoyed more son-and-mother moments with her than he had with his own mother, who had delegated the chore of raising him but retained the official name of their bond.

'No. Pretty big guy, all dressed in black, plastic shoe covers on.' 'With the combine?'

'Yeah, he bashed me about a bit, tied me up, then set it in gear to mow me down before scarpering.'

'How did you get away?' 'Narrowly, let's put it that way.'

A moment's silence passed. The baby cooed, and Thor automatically jiggled his knee.

'You don't think one of us lot did it, do you?' she said.

'I honestly don't know, sis. I'm not Mr. Popular around here, I know that much.'

'But murder, Thor—murder. Think about what you are saying. Look, we are all set in our ways to some degree, even you, though you're too bolshy to admit it, but murder?'

'I know, Rue.'

'You're sure it wasn't a prank gone wrong?'

'If it was a prank they got me good and proper. A for effort.'

'But, who would want you dead? What have you been up to since you left here? Seriously?' Rue leaned closer, while Andrew burbled to bring the focus of the conversation back to him.

'I have no idea, Rue. None. But I've been thinking. You know why I left, right? You must have guessed by now.'

'Assume I'm as thickheaded as Otter and Beaver and give it me in your words.'

Thor chose his words carefully. He had mulled over his reasons for months, and now he wanted to sound justified.

'It was that stupid Loxley tradition—the one Dad was so obsessed with. It was the assumption that I'd go along with it.'

'Which one, Thor? There are a few of those.'

There were Loxley traditions that ranged from the order of Christmas present opening to the cracking of the first egg at breakfast in the morning. Every morning. Every single one of them felt pointless to Thor.

'I think someone tried to kill me in that particular field because it's

my field. The one I own.'

Rue leaned back, the implications suddenly clear. Any one of their siblings, and their parents, had real reason to be upset with Thor because of how he had handled his inheritance—the field.

Eight generations earlier, the first Wilkes Loxley had decided to take an active hand in the lives of his children and involve them in the running of the family farm, by giving them an incentive. He gave each of his offspring, when they came of age (deemed oddly by the first Wilkes to be age twenty-three), a piece of the farm's land. He signed the deeds over to them on the assumption that they would be bequeathed at the end to the next Wilkes for the next Loxley generation, and so the cycle would continue.

It was expected that the recipient could decide roughly what direction to take his or her land in, but importantly, within the limits of the prosperity of the farm as a whole. You could decide to put potatoes in it for example, and you'd get a carefully worked out cut of the farm's profits according to how well it did.

The system was designed to give responsibility to the next generation of Loxleys, as well as to promote teamwork and unity among the siblings, who often teamed up. The competitive atmosphere often enhanced the strength of the farm, and prosperity ensued.

Thor didn't see it like that, and had always dreaded the moment he was to be given his allocated piece of land.

He had felt like an afterthought all his life. And his own piece of land had been hacked out accordingly— a field on the margins, and of lesser worth than others. That had left Thor feeling lost, and, paradoxically, personally misused. The name Loxley was bandied about like a golden ticket at home, not to mention in Crook's Hollow itself, but as he reached the age of eligibility, Thor felt the family more and more as a ball and chain. He felt shackled to a life and legacy he felt no part of, and then the piece of land came along and he was expected to follow obediently.

The problem with the land gift was that, in Thor's mind, it was self- serving. It didn't seem to have anything to do with charity or even with family wealth. It seemed to be designed to do nothing more than consolidate the farm while appearing to be progressive, generous, and pro-family.

So when the time came for Thor to receive the land gift, and put his land back into the family pot, he voted with his feet: he didn't do anything with it. He had a plan—a long game. The field was on the edge of the Loxley land, pushed out to the edges and framed by hedges and a main road. He liked the access. He wanted to build a home on it, and try to work as much of it as he could by himself. It became a dream, a chance to finagle a silver lining from what he'd always felt was his low ranking in the family.

But when his father heard his plan, he hit the roof. It didn't fit in with the purpose of the tradition, nor unify the family's wealth. They fell out in grand terms. So, Thor let the field go fallow, then wild, and stubbornly refused to allow it to be used for anything. It became a dead spot of land, a stubborn statement of his refusal to participate in his own family's prosperity.

He knew it was immature. He knew it was stupid. But Thor's name was on the deeds, and the field was his—his family couldn't touch it. And so began the standoff between Thor and his father, two years festering and counting.

Rue knew the history, and needed no introduction to it.

'Thor, what happened is unfortunate, and in so many ways still is; but do you really think any Loxley would lay a finger on you? I know you're not dead keen on the Loxley name, but we Loxley's don't have a habit of harming our own—and we all know how much sway family history has around here.'

Thor could see the point, but he had finally established a possible motive for the attack, and it was impossible to ignore.

'I just don't know, Rue. I'm beginning to realise that digging my heels in and behaving like a bit of a snotty little shit wasn't the smartest move.'

'Well, any one of us could have told you that ages ago, you bleeding retard.'

Rue put her arm on her younger brother's shoulder. 'The best you can do now, in all seriousness, is to get Mum and Dad involved. There are differences between you, of course, but if there's anything that

Loxleys are especially good at, it's going off all us against the world. They'll know what to do and how to handle it.'

'Maybe,' Thor conceded. He didn't really want to have to go cap in hand to his parents, and admit that maybe he had been a bit silly about the whole land thing and that maybe he should have been a good boy—even if it was just a means to an end. But if it kept him safe and well, and helped him find out who attacked him, then maybe it was the only sensible course of action.

'Have you involved the police?' asked Rue.

'Not yet. I'm hoping I won't have to. In house, remember.'

'Forgive me Thor, but sod all that. Someone tried to kill you, for crying out loud.' Rue's voice rose just enough to upset little Andrew, who was confused at his mother's change in tone. He reached for her and Thor handed him over, while thinking to himself that maybe Rue was right and getting justice officially was a much better tactic.

But was that what Thor wanted? Justice? How was he going to deliver that without involving the police?

In house was one thing, but escalating what had happened would quickly become an eye for an eye— and he didn't want that either. Like the stubborn mule he was, he had gone headlong into finding out who wanted to hurt him without thinking about what he'd do when he eventually did.

The atmosphere in the small, dark kitchen began to close in on Thor. He had never liked being forced to make a choice which he had been corralled towards; that wasn't the point of a decision. But it was exactly the problem which had started this whole escapade, and it could be the very thing that had a chance of ending it. He had, however, one last question.

'What do you think? Who do you think did it?'

Rue, without blinking, began to undo her top. Thor knew it was only natural and normal, but it still caught him off guard whenever she did it in his presence. He turned respectfully to one side, and fixed his eyes out of the window. A slurp and a gurgle later, and Andrew was latched onto Rue and feeding greedily.

'I don't know,' she said. 'But there is one family who have always gone to great pains to make life difficult for us.'

Thor met her gaze. He knew who she was referring to without even giving voice to their name. And silently, there was the added complication that Roisin, the wonderful, down-to-earth girl he was falling for, carried that exact same name.

But then Thor remembered what Wendell had said earlier that day, when he bragged that they had done something that would really piss Thor's dad off. Those were his words, and Thor couldn't ignore them, nor the timing of the claim.

'Wendell Crook said he and Ward had done something that would really upset Dad.'

This raised Rue's hackles to the point where Andrew lost his feeding rhythm. Noticing, she settled him back down immediately.

'Well, that would give me all the suggestion I'd need to look to them for answers.' Rage seemed to make her cheeks glow.

The battle between the Loxleys and the Crooks dated back to the very beginning of Crook's Hollow.

The original Crook's Farm was established just one year before the first Loxley settlement, in 1751. A solitary year might mean nothing to damn near everyone else, but to the Loxleys and the Crooks it was everything. Both farms were prosperous and, both being arable farms, competitive, and it didn't help things that their properties abutted: at the north end of the village, the two dynasties were separated by nothing more than a long hedge full of appropriately sour gooseberries.

That one year was a constant sticking point. The Crooks felt the Hollow was theirs in more than just name, but the fact that the Loxleys had just that tiny bit more square acreage gave them all the fuel they needed to claim preeminence. And thus a grudge was borne which came to characterise not just each and every member of the two families through the generations, but the village of Crook's Hollow as well.

Somewhere else in the bungalow, an old cuckoo clock croaked what might once have been a jaunty morning song.

'What time is it?' Thor asked.

Rue checked her watch. 'One thirty.'

Thor got up. He needed to get a bit of perspective on the conclusions they had reached, but he also felt a nagging need to find out what Lionel Clyne had been harping on about in the field earlier. That 'meeting' at the parish hall was fast approaching.

'You couldn't give me a ride into the Hollow shortly, could you?' 'Safer than letting you go anywhere alone, it seems,' Rue said.

Again she reached out and took Thor's hand. It felt weird, with her so exposed by feeding Andrew. 'Promise me you'll not do anything stupid,' Rue said.

Thor forgot about his awkwardness and looked at his sister, and felt a resurgence of the love and admiration for her he had always carried. He felt like shit for being distant for nearly two years—Rue deserved better.

'I will,' he replied, 'but please keep this to yourself.'

Rue nodded once, and squeezed his hand so hard that Thor felt for the first time since last night that things might just turn out OK after all.

13

Rue's blue minivan pulled into the parish hall car park just as the first drops of rain began to patter the windshield. The car park was half full, with people still arriving behind them. In the parking bay nearest the front door stood, sure enough, the black Range Rover Thor saw after he and Roisin had encountered Lionel Clyne and his friends.

'You have any idea what this is about?' asked Rue. 'Sunday afternoons, the hall's usually reserved for Bitch 'n' Stitch.'

Thor glanced at Rue in surprise, and she smiled and explained: 'It's the nickname they gave the weekly knitting-slash-gossip meeting.'

'I've no idea, I'm afraid, but I was asked by the owner of that big carbon footprint to attend.' Thor gestured to the Range.

'You sure that's wise?' Rue asked. 'I don't really know.'

'Oh, there she is…' said Rue, looking towards the churchyard at the right of the hall. Weaving between the headstones was the bobbing dark hair of Roisin. 'I think I'll leave you to it.'

'You don't have to go,' Thor said. 'You'd like her, I'd bet the farm on

it.'

Rue smiled. 'Sure you would. I'm more progressive than most

Loxleys… but I need to get back. The rest of the kids will be home soon and I need to get ready for the next round of parental chaos.'

Thor nodded, thanked her, and got out. He had texted Roisin to ask her to be there, but to defuse any gossip they had agreed to sit apart before convening afterwards to swap their thoughts.

Roisin saw him, gave a smile and a wink, and Thor wanted for all the world to hold her hand and walk in with her. Forget what anyone else thinks. Get on with living their lives and let things play out naturally, without pressure. Instead he watched her enter alone and shamelessly eyed her denim-clad backside as it disappeared into the hall.

He waited a full minute in the rain before following her.

The hall had changed not at all since Thor's youth. Even the chairs were the same: chipped pine with a faded floral vinyl seat cushion. The floor would once have been a fairly ornate parquet, but it was now so scuffed and scarred that it looked more like set mud than anything resembling wood. Overhead was a whitewashed convex roof that Thor knew was stuffed to the brim with asbestos, but funding simply didn't exist to do anything about it. Thor had been to the hall many times as a youth, for the quick-fix birthday parties of his friends, indoor football training, karate for a short while, and Cubs, but those did literally nothing but scratch the surface of just how many groups and activities had graced the hall over the years.

Today at the front stood a tall easel with a huge piece of card on it, blank. A table stood to the side, entrenched by a set of chairs. Before them were set out rows and rows of seating in two columns, right to the back. As before, he recognised many of the people milling around waiting for things to start. Ties had been taken off from the earlier visit to church, and raincoats had been added.

Roisin had picked a row on the front right, so Thor picked one in the middle on the far left. He sat down and listened to the murmur of voices around him. He had never once craved gossip, but he felt from the murmur that he had missed a trick by keeping out of it, because from what he could hear, everyone seemed to have a nervous idea of what was going on. And the word on everyone's lips seemed to be 'development.' The old couple in front of him who he recognised from the pub (he appearing on Friday afternoons after work, she appearing at half six to drag him halfheartedly home) were leaning into each other but Thor could hear their conversation, thanks to the fact that neither of them could evidently hear properly, so their words weren't exactly whispered.

'Have they started yet?' he said to her.

'The papers said they needed permission first,' she answered. 'But they said the council were in favour of it so they shouldn't find it hard to get that.'

'I hope they don't bloody do it.'

'If they do, we'll need a bigger Sainsburys.'

Thor had a feeling in his gut that he couldn't place, but if the couple were on the right lines, he certainly didn't like what he was hearing. Developments had sprung up in nearer villages, and he was not the only one who had been relieved that it hadn't happened in the Hollow. Maybe that was about to change.

At the side of the room was a hatch for a strip-lit, dank kitchen, with an adjoining, half open door—and looking over, Thor nearly did a double take. The small group of people drinking tea in the kitchen were the three from the field, and they had been joined by others. There must have been five or six of them.

Someone cleared his throat, and the crowd quieted all at once, as crowds do. At the front stood the well-known figure of David Campbell, committee leader for the parish, and he was raising a hand.

Campbell was average in every possible way: average height, average build, noncommittal brown hair, and non-offensive average features—neither a catalogue model, nor a troll. He just… was. And he'd been a feature of village life for all of his fifty-five years. His brother Martin was the pub landlord and Thor's boss, and Thor had seen him many times in his youth at Loxley Farm, on matters both business and social.

'OK, ladies and gentlemen, I know we all want to get home to our Sunday roasts but it's important we give our visitors our ears. Please can I welcome to Crook's Hollow, Lionel Clyne and the team from COMUDEV.' He pronounced the team name com-you-dev, in such a way that it sounded strangely like the name of a Soviet video-game developer.

Campbell clapped, but only a couple of other people did. Thor looked across the hall to see that the rows had filled out. It was well attended.

The door to the kitchen opened fully, and out came Clyne, taking the lead. There was laughter amongst the small party as they filed out, which served to establish a feeling of disconnect between the two groups. It felt as though a group of the high and mighty gentry were in town to take a gander at the serfs.

'Thank you, David, thank you!' said Clyne with the delivery of a travelling ringmaster, as he arrived at the front and his companions took the seats around him.

'Can I introduce you to the team at COMUDEV, who have been working with me tirelessly to bring good things to the region - your region.' Clyne introduced each one of them in turn, but Thor didn't hear a word. He was transfixed by what was on the easel card one of the suits had reached over and turned around.

It was a map of the Hollow, which Thor recognised immediately. But in the middle, a garish red shape appeared. It looked like a new border. A border within the outline. Around the edges of the map were artists' renderings of small domiciles, each one roughly quaint but tiny. It was a plan for a housing development, right in the middle of

Crook's Hollow.

Thor was stunned. He followed the outline of the red border. He saw the centre of the village at the bottom of the map, safely away from the main, red shape. He saw his family's land on the top right, and the Crook's land on the upper left. The red shape was in the space in between. It overlapped quite a bit on the Crook side, but only one bit on the Loxley side. And the bit that it overlay was clearly the field in which Thor was attacked last night. Thor's parcel of land. It was Thor's field.

Clyne and COMUDEV wanted to build on his land.

Thor looked over for Roisin. This development would affect both their families in a huge way, and his mind was swimming. Sure enough, Roisin was staring at the image, her own eyes wide with shock and confusion. Their worlds had just been turned upside down, and Thor wanted more than anything to reach out to her, to touch her.

He looked back to the front. The development would double the population of the village, easily. It would change everybody's lives. It would change Crook's Hollow forever.

He noticed that Clyne was frequently making eye contact with him, and it dawned on Thor that it was no wonder Clyne had wanted him to attend. He wanted Thor's land, and this was a sales pitch, just for him.

Thor wracked his brain to work out how Clyne would know that that parcel on the map on the Loxley side was his. Not that Thor was particularly au fait with legal matters such as these, but he reasoned that his ownership must be a matter of public record. Thor himself had told nobody, the whole subject still very sore and private to him, but he couldn't guarantee that his siblings hadn't done the same. There were four of them, not counting Rue, and he was on poor terms with all of them. Could one of them have spilled the beans to these developers?

In fact, thought Thor, where in God's name were they? Surely plans for a development could have a huge bearing on the Loxleys' lives. And yet none of them were here to hear the proposal.

And, for that matter, where were the Crooks? Their land, according to the developers' map, was even more affected than the Loxleys', and any plan going forward would have to rely on their agreement.

The fact that both the village's most rooted families were absent suggested to Thor that he was missing something.

Thor glanced around the room. His boss was there, as was Ahmed. Of course they would be here—this kind of thing would hugely impact their businesses. They may even support it.

Thor turned back to the front. Clyne was speaking.

'… jobs, of course. With increased amenities would come increased work opportunities. And with increased work opportunities comes improved overall prosperity in the region. Crook's Hollow would become a better place to live because of it.'

The silence which greeted that statement led Thor to believe that not many people agreed with it. Thor knew the village and its people. Change wasn't always greeted with open arms.

'And if you think of the potential for improvement to the current local facilities—yes?' Clyne was looking at someone in the centre of the room.

'Can I ask a question?'

Thor recognised the speaker, he lived on the 1960s estate— ironically the last time major development was brought to Crook's Hollow.

Clyne smiled broadly in response.

'There was going to be a Q and A at the end, but of course, let's hear it! I want to show that we are not just another set of faceless developers that you read about in the more hysterical tabloids.'

The man stood. 'How many homes, in total, are you hoping to build here?'

Clyne glanced back at one of the suits behind him—the woman who had been in the field with him earlier. Her precisely coiffured hair jiggled once in a swift nod.

'Approximately one thousand five hundred,' said Clyne.

A gasp swept the room, as the gravity and scale of the proposal hit home for the first time. The man who'd asked the question, however, retained his composure.

'And I assume you want to create a new road infrastructure, to cope with such a demand?'

Clyne answered immediately.

'We believe the existing road structure will be just fine. The entrances to the site would be placed on the roads as they are.'

Silence greeted this, but Thor understood the implication. If each house was at least a one-car household, with many being two, you were looking at total daily gridlock across the entirety of the village. It would be day-to-day traffic bedlam.

'What about the school?' a woman's voice all but shouted. It was the headmistress of the village primary. 'We have only got a hundred and eighty pupils and that's full as it is!'

'We will look into extending it. It will all be taken care of,' Clyne crooned. He gave a smile of impossibly pearly whites which suggested to Thor that taking care of any such thing was right at the back of his mind.

Voices began to erupt around the hall, and Thor could only pick out odd bleats in the hubbub.

'Affordable housing? Does that mean council houses?' 'Will council tax come down?'

'Will this mean the potholes will be filled in?'

The woman in front of Thor piped up: 'We'll need a bigger Sainsburys!'

'What does the council say?'

Clyne opted to answer the last one, using an up-and-down motion of his arms to try to quiet the audience down.

'The council know of the proposal, of course. And they are in full support of it. I can say that unequivocally. This is in partnership with them. Bringing affordable homes to the area is something that was promised by the council some time ago, and this has emerged as the most suitable site. It is win-win.'

'Where are they then?' someone shouted.

Where indeed? If the council were in on it, surely they would show their faces, or at least be represented. Thor felt sure that the reason for the no-show was a bottle job. They didn't have the backbone to face the residents on a matter which they were both directly involved with and which affected their public so wholly.

'Would you live there?' someone else shouted, which was answered with a snort by one of the suits behind Clyne. Clyne glanced back sharply, but that told Thor all he needed to know about the whole sorry affair. He couldn't wait to get out, and find his own answers.

14

As soon as Thor got outside, he threw caution to the wind. He found Roisin and held her tight to him. They didn't care anymore, and as it turned out, neither did anyone else.

'Did you know?' asked Thor into her hair.

'No,' she whispered to his chest. 'I can't believe it.'

'Where are our families? I can't believe they are not here.'

Roisin was clearly on the same wavelength. 'It could change everything, for them both. And us.'

Thor could only nod grimly, thinking about the one piece of Loxley land that would have to be sold for COMUDEV's plans to move forward - his.

'We need to see them. You go see yours, and I'll go see mine,' Thor said. He watched the people feed out of the parish hall. There was an overall tone that suggested Lionel Clyne was the harbinger of the end times. 'How did you get here?'

'Car's parked on the other side of the church. Couldn't park any closer.'

'Could you give me a ride back to yours to pick up my car?'

'Of course,' Roisin said quickly, linking her fingers through his. It was the first time they had held hands in public. It felt really good; Thor just wished the circumstances were happier.

They passed through the graveyard, along the path that Thor had walked only that morning. He patted Ma Loxley's grave just as a loud rumbling arose nearby. Thor looked around. He couldn't see anything, but the roar was growing in intensity.

And then it happened.

A car smashed through the first row of tombstones, sending them tumbling like dominos in all directions. Chunks of turf sailed over the car's windshield, obscuring identification of the driver. The engine's roar was deafening as it careened straight at Thor, but Thor's only thought was for Roisin. She screamed his name and he gave her one mighty shove to the side, just before Ma Loxley's gravestone was upended and spat at Thor with so much force that when it hit him, he was catapulted out onto the grass, out of the direction of the careening vehicle.

He landed with an awful thud, the wind blasted clean out of his lungs, and the last thing he saw as he lay in the dirt, consciousness slipping away for the second time that day, was silver hubcaps tinged with rust as they pounded through the graveyard just a foot from his face.

15

Thor awoke to the sound of someone throwing up. His eyes inched open reluctantly, as if there were a harsh reality to accept on waking fully. His last thoughts before blackness hadn't been good—what the hell had happened to him? And what about Roisin? All he remembered was flying dirt and flipping tombstones.

Like ripping off a plaster, he forced his eyes open in a quick burst. He was in near darkness, lying in a bed with a cream woolen blanket around him. The bed was completely encircled by floor-to-ceiling curtains, and he could hear snoring from somewhere off to his left, which was a welcome respite to the sound of retching. He looked down: two arms, two legs. He was relieved to appear to be in one piece. 'Hello, Mr Loxley,' said a man with such a deep soothing voice Thor thought he could well still be in dreamland. He turned to the direction of it and winced as something in his neck caught painfully. It felt like a thin wire down the centre of his neck was grazing a razor

blade.

'Take it easy. You are in Warrington Hospital. You've had a bit of an accident.'

The voice was clipped by an accent Thor couldn't place. 'No shit,' he said, in a weak, strangled voice. The man was sitting at the end of the bed, on a chair in the corner of the curtain box. 'Is Roisin OK?'

There was a moment's silence, as the outline of the man came into better focus. He was a well-built black man in a blue three-piece suit.

'Roisin Crook is fine. The women's ward along the hall is where she's resting for the night. She's fine, just very, very shook up. I'm Detective Sergeant Okpara, Greater Manchester Police.'

Okpara pulled his chair closer and Thor could see him better in the low orange light of the glowing nurse call button. He was immaculately presented, carefully manicured. Wire frame glasses over expressive brown eyes, his hair a neat crop with a beard the same length, giving the impression of a precise wraparound balaclava of hair.

'You sit watching people in the dark often, Okpara?' Thor blustered—a growing habit of his in these ever more tense times. Despite his efforts, the police had now got involved, and it made him uneasy.

Okpara smiled and took out his identification, placing it on the bed next to Thor's hand. Thor let his eyes flick to it, but nothing more. He saw the detective's image next to a shield and that was enough for him. 'The doctors assure me you will be fine, although you did take a

nasty bump,' said Okpara.

'Who was driving the car?' Thor asked.

'We were hoping you would know. The eyewitnesses we interviewed in the churchyard said that the car didn't stop once, it just came off the road, ploughed through that corner of the graveyard, and bounced into the car park. Sprayed some people with gravel then sped back off down the drive.'

To Thor, it sounded less and less like an accident, but Okpara was ahead of him. 'The witnesses did confirm, however, that the driver was wearing a full mask, with only the eyes visible. And that says to me that this was planned. So I have to ask you, Mr.

Loxley, do you know of anyone who would try to cause you harm?'

The question that had dominated the last forty-eight hours. Thor had no real aversion to police, but it had been ingrained in him to deal with things without involving outsiders, especially law enforcement. What goes on on your own farm was your territory and your business. That's how it has always been done in parts like these.

Now Thor had to decide whether to come clean about the incident the night before as well. But if Okpara had already spoken to Roisin, he might already know. It would all depend on what Roisin had said.

'Mr Loxley,' continued Okpara, 'I understand that moments like these do carry a weight of shock. It's important that you take the time to heal mentally, but it is equally important that if this was a deliberate attempt to hurt you, that we get the search for your attacker underway. So, if you feel up to speaking with me, then I'd like to help and I'm all ears. If you don't, please take some time and we will find a more suitable moment. But, in my experience, waiting too long will make justice harder to come by.'

Okpara was so measured and steady, his actions and demeanour so calming, yet firm. They instilled confidence, hope, trust and calm. He was simply a magnetic presence.

'Have you spoken with Roisin?' Thor asked. 'I have. Again, she is fine.'

'What did she say? Did she see anything?'

Okpara smiled balefully. 'I'm afraid the answer to both of those questions is the same. Nothing. She was desperate to help, but saw nothing and hadn't a clue who would try to hurt you.'

Thor felt warm inside at the thought of Roisin's loyalty. She had remembered he had left the police out of it, and had stuck to that line rigidly. He smiled despite himself.

'I love her,' he said.

Okpara smiled, more positively this time. 'You both are very lucky. The distinct impression I get is that your feelings aren't a one-way street.'

Again, Thor felt heartened and elated, amongst all sorts of warring thoughts. The attempted hit and run could have killed them both, and if it weren't for Thor shoving Roisin out of harm's way, and Ma Loxley's tombstone effectively doing the same to Thor, neither would be here to have any feelings for each other at all.

There was a future there, if Thor was brave enough to take it. But there had already been two attempts on his life, and they had ramped up in intensity. He didn't want to give his pursuers a third try, not now they were clearly happy to put Roisin in the firing line with him.

Thor would have to come clean with Okpara if he wanted to improve his chances of safety, and Okpara had won him round to

wanting to speak up.

'Someone tried to kill me last night too,' Thor said in a whisper. 'In a field near my home.'

Okpara blinked once in surprise, but quickly regained his composure. 'Please go on, Mr Loxley. Start at the beginning.'

Thor told him all about the attack the night before, and what he remembered from the attempt that afternoon, and the detective made the occasional note on a pad.

By the end, Okpara had a furrowed brow and his eyes were roving his notes fervently, flicking the pages of his notebook back and forth like a jumbled flip-book.

'I'll make some enquiries, Mr Loxley, but in the meantime this is the best place for you. I'll get a uniform stationed on the ward, and see if we can have you moved to a private room. Thank you for telling me your story, and if you can think of anything else, the nurses' station has my details.'

Okpara left and Thor slumped, numb for a bit, before relief slowly seeped in through his toes. He wasn't shouldering the burden quite so alone anymore, and for the first time since yesterday, he felt optimistic and even safe.

Or so he thought.

16

The phone was answered before the first ring had even finished. 'Yes?' A whisper.

'Are you alone?' the caller asked.

'I can be.' A moment passed, over which the hissing void of the phone line carried the rustling of bed sheets. 'OK.'

'It didn't work.'

'Jesus. Loxley's like teflon.'

'No names over the phone,' the caller said. 'Sorry.'

'At least now he's in one place. We need another go. Can it be arranged?'

'I'll look into it.'

The caller's voice grew urgent. 'It needs to be soon.' 'Like I said, I'll look into it.'

'You do that. I've got to go.'

The line went dead. The person who'd been called stood there, listening to the dial tone, staring into space, contemplating the scale of their next challenge, before shutting the phone off.

17

The ward came to life at the stroke of dawn. Grey light beat through the windows as hard rain pummeled their panes. Thor kept the curtains around the bed shut, and just lay there, listening. For some strange reason, the steady drumming, blocking out interior sounds, was loud enough to give the illusion of privacy.

The doctor had been in at first light and confirmed that Thor had bruised ribs and a mild concussion. Thor told her about the neck pain, and she said that would soon dissipate with painkillers. Thor popped the few that she had prescribed him, and lay there waiting for them to kick in.

He felt alone, and, in a way he hated himself for, abandoned. A young fellow his age should have all sorts of family checking on his well-being, but there had been nothing. Again, he felt let down by his parents. Whether the police had communicated the incident to them or not, the village grapevine would have sown the information wide enough for them to hear. There were enough witnesses at the church, for crying out loud. If they gave a shit, he thought, he would have heard from them by now.

Unless, of course, they were behind the whole thing.

Thor eventually found out from the nurse that visiting hours began at ten a.m., just for an hour until eleven. Whether he would be allowed visitors or not was unclear, considering the ward was supposed to be under surveillance by a police officer.

In his mind, in between bouts of furtive sleep during the night, he had looked at his list of possible suspects again, and tried to work out who precisely would gain from his death.

Aside from the prospect of the land development, nothing had changed. The list was the same. But the big money prospect of the value of his land and its importance in the overall picture of COMUDEV's plans brought a new suspect to mind: Lionel Clyne.

Thor almost dismissed it out of hand, because the risk to Clyne was so great. But if Thor was out of the picture, the housing development could surely take one step closer.

Thor poured himself some water. The painkillers had worked, and his neck felt better with every passing moment, but that didn't stop his head from pounding. He knew it wasn't the concussion either. Since the meeting yesterday at the parish hall, everything looked different but somehow still the same. He felt he could cross a few people off his list, but he couldn't be sure. It all depended on what the Crooks and Loxleys knew of the housing development plans on their land— something he intended to find out. He couldn't picture that either family would allow it, and it would be a case of such things happening over certain people's dead bodies. And if they were against the project, then Thor was far more useful to them all alive. As long as he was alive and refused to sell his land, then the development couldn't progress regardless of how much Clyne blustered.

But that left Clyne looking ever more like being the main beneficiary of Thor's death. Then again, he stood as the party with the most to lose. The bigger they are, the harder they fall.

On the other hand, maybe the attacks had nothing to do with the land at all. You should have got on with it. What did it mean? Was the land issue a smoke screen for something else entirely?

Thor could hear the breakfast trolley being wheeled to other patients. He still hadn't opened the curtains since he woke to Okpara last night, opting to relieve himself in the little cardboard bottle by his bed instead. He didn't know how many other patients were in the ward with him.

He knew very little about where he was, save for the fact that he knew it was Warrington Hospital, but ground floor, top floor, what wing, what ward—all that was a mystery to him. As the questions mounted inexorably around him like sandbags of doubt, he began to feel more and more trapped, and increasingly wary.

Amongst all the circling what-if's was one big concrete fact, cemented in place by Okpara's visit: whoever had tried to kill him was still out there. And the longer he was stuck here, the more he became a sitting duck, protection or no protection. Besides, Roisin was stuck in a ward somewhere nearby too. If they wanted to get to him, they could go after her.

He didn't like it. At all.

What were his options? Sit tight, and wait for Okpara to do his job and make his enquiries? Thor knew just how the community would receive him, and it filled him with little confidence. The stubborn streak in him begged for an audience, and it told him he could get more done by himself.

He couldn't stay there. Staying there, with a wannabe killer at large, was suicide. And if he left, then his adversaries would be on the back foot, not knowing where he'd got to.

He had to get out of there. As soon as possible.

18

Visiting hour came and went with no visitors. It surprised Thor in precisely no way, so he focused instead on a plan to escape, and most importantly, how he was going to get past the policeman on the door.

He had been stripped out of his clothes, which had then been dry cleaned and folded in the wooden locker by his bed. His wallet, keys, and phone, blank-screened thanks to its battery running down, sat on top of them. He had been dressed in a backless gown with demeaning paper knickers, and tried not to think of how or when that had happened. The nurse said he had been awake for a bit when he came in, not that he could remember any of that.

As soon as it hit eleven o'clock, he got up and dressed. He winced as he pulled his t-shirt on, but overall he felt pretty good. His neck was fine now, and his head even felt clearer than it had done in days.

Fully clothed, he did a sweep of the room. He was going to pretend he needed the loo, and try to engineer a diversion somehow, but before he could take another step, the curtain swished open.

Thor turned, expecting to explain himself to a nurse, but was stunned to see Lionel Clyne standing there. Clyne looked resplendent in a black suit with an open-necked white shirt, his face clean shaven with wrinkles that he'd adopted as his own rather than try to hide— which looked to be about the only natural thing about his appearance. He beamed at Thor, who stared back at him with wide eyes.

'Mr Loxley, I'm so glad to see you're alright. God, what a terrible accident.'

'How did you get in here?' Thor said, backing up to the bed, his mind bolting. With no will, the field would end up for sale, in would swing Clyne and COMUDEV. The man who would benefit most from Thor's death was right here in his hospital ward.

'I . . . walked?' Clyne replied, answering Thor's own question with a question of his own.

'There's supposed to be a policeman on the door.'
'Well, there isn't now.'

Thor felt the thinly veiled menace in Clyne's words, but he couldn't tell if he was just being paranoid. Where the hell was that policeman?

'Visiting just finished,' Thor said, gathering his wallet, phone, and keys and putting them in his pocket. He was not planning to hang about.

'I asked them for just two minutes, given how close I was to arriving.'

'And they just let you have that, did they?'

'It's surprising what you can get if you ask nicely.'

'Have you ever thought of asking me what you want to know—

nicely?'

Clyne smiled, showing his pearly whites.

'I really do like you, you know. You're so direct, it's refreshing. I usually just deal with yes men. You know, yes sir, no sir, three bags full, sir. You certainly make things far more interesting.'

'I know what you want, Clyne.'

Clyne's eyes narrowed. 'Do you? Do you really?'

'My land. You want my field for your little building project.' 'That would be nice, yes. Do you fancy giving it to me?'

'You're a slippery customer, Clyne. What I fancy is telling you to fuck off.'

Clyne laughed. 'And there he goes again. I did picture you'd feel something like that, although I could never have put it as succinctly.' He reached into his jacket pocket, causing Thor to tense visibly. 'Calm down, Mr Loxley. If I was going to do something stupid, I definitely wouldn't do it here.'

Thor's eyes widened at the prospect. It certainly seemed that this snake was the man behind his problems, so much so that he was almost toying with Thor.

Clyne pulled his hand out, and in it was a piece of paper—a cheque.

'I'm so grateful that you came to the meeting yesterday. I hope you can see what it is I'm trying to achieve with the Crook's Hollow project. Affordable homes are such a big requirement these days in the development sector, and as the UK economy continues to flounder like a drunk lying in a pool of his own vomit, that necessity is more pressing than ever. We can do real good in Crook's Hollow—

together. Please see this gesture as an attempt to get you on my side.'

Thor glanced down at the cheque. It was made out to him for 1.2 million pounds. Thor's knees felt suddenly weak.

'A bribe,' he said.

'Not a bribe at all! That's for the purchase of your field. I did a land registry search, I know it's in your name. That's what I'll give you for it.'

'You want to buy it off me?'

Thor stared at the cheque, unable almost to look away. It would change his whole life... but his family would despise him forever. If there was a future to make things up with his family, it would be lost if he accepted.

Words would hardly come, but he tried his best to tap into his bravado. 'Bit of a change of tactic for you, this.'

Clyne cocked a perfectly shaped eyebrow. 'We all try to get where we are going the best way we know how.'

'Cut the bollocks. You think, after trying to have me killed, you can just pay your way out of it?'

Clyne threw his head back and laughed. 'Oh dear. The bump on your head must be worse than we thought. I'll get the nurse in here.'

'Answer the question, you wrinkled old shit.'

The bite in Thor's words seemed to make Clyne hesitate.

'Take the cheque,' he said. 'Keep it for a couple of days. And think long and hard about what it means for you if you accept, and what it means for you if you don't. Forty-eight hours from now, I cancel the cheque, and things may get a lot less civilised. You cash the cheque in the meantime, and I'll assume we have a deal and I'll send a notary over to you with some papers to sign. You're above the post office, I believe?'

Thor remained silent.

'Gosh, that place is going to get so much busier,' said Clyne.

Thor had heard enough. He needed to get out, find Roisin, and speak to his family, and he couldn't bear another minute of Clyne's presence. The guy gave him the creeps with his goading riddles and his arrogance, not to mention that Thor was now sure

Clyne had tried to have him killed, not once but twice, and was brazen enough to visit his quarry in hospital with a different attempt at getting his own way.

Clyne had said there was no policeman on the door—and that was enough to push Thor into action. Shoving Clyne aside, he ran from the curtained cubicle and headed for the door, leaving Clyne with a surprised smile on his face. Thor could see no PC on the other side of the door, so he bounded through at speed. Out into the hallway, he was facing a long corridor bathed in insipid halogen, with a nurses' station to his left and double doors to his right.

In an instant, he chose right, and burst through the double doors. His mind was fixed on Roisin and getting to her, but he knew he didn't have much time. What was it Okpara said?

The women's ward along the hall.

He ran past some vending machines, doors he guessed opened on private rooms, and a group of people in street clothes leaving another set of double doors. Thor thought that must be another ward. He got to the doors just as the last person was ushered out by a nurse. Seeing Thor, she held her hand up.

'Hang on, no more visitors, it took me donkey's years just to get this lot out.' She wore a weary, hangdog expression.

'Roisin Crook, is she in there?' Thor asked, panting. 'Who are you?'

'Her… boyfriend.' They'd never had the discussion of putting a formal name to their relationship, but despite how awkward it felt, Thor found himself enjoying saying it, plus he knew it would get results.

'Well, boyfriend, Miss Crook was discharged this morning.'

That stopped Thor stone dead, but he knew he couldn't stay. 'Thanks,' he said before running down the corridor. He was confused. Confused that he didn't know. It made him worry—surely she would have tried to contact him? But then he remembered that his phone was dead.

He needed to get out of there, then he needed a phone charger, and he needed to call her. Only when they were together, and he could see she was OK, would he feel safe. Because he damn well didn't feel safe in here. Would he feel safe at home? He doubted it. But at least out there he could hide out, and turn enough rocks over to reveal something which would tie Clyne to the attempts on his life.

19

Thor took a taxi from the hospital back to Crook's Hollow, which cost him twelve quid. He wouldn't usually spring for something like that, not with a bus service he could hop on to for a fraction of the cost, but with a cheque for 1.2 million in his pocket, he felt a bit flush.

The Hollow was situated almost exactly in between the two cities of Manchester and Liverpool, and about five miles from Warrington itself. It took about twenty-five minutes of stop-start Monday lunchtime traffic. Not to mention, it was heaving cats and dogs, and the roadways were so awash he could probably have Jet Ski'd home, given the chance.

'Have you ever seen anything like this?' asked the cabbie in a thick Liverpudlian twang.

'Never,' Thor replied. 'You think they'll be right? The reports of flooding?'

'It's town I worry about. The River Mersey runs right through it.' The driver said Mersey like a

Frenchman might say thank you. 'The villages will be fine because there's no large bodies of running water to overflow.'

That made Thor feel better; after all, there was no better source of information than the humble cabbie.

When they got to Crook's Hollow, after some idle chit-chat about football teams (the cabbie was a red from Manchester, Thor a red from Liverpool, yet they somehow managed not to come to blows), Thor got out at The Traveller's Rest. He took the rear entrance next to the car park, away from any eyes that might catch him going in the front.

As he entered the back bar, once the Smoker's Bar before the EU decided they'd had quite enough of that, he saw the old Guinness clock over the dartboard reading 12:03. The bar itself was double sided, with one side for the back bar, a small door, and then the main lounge on the other. It let the same barman, usually Thor, cater for both sides, and it was split accordingly. Locals in the back, tourists in the front.

Martin Campbell came through from the front, and proceeded to empty a bowl of dry roasted nuts into a dish by the door frame, which he nibbled on throughout the day like a sparrow at a garden feeder. He jumped when he caught sight of Thor.

'Christ, I thought you were one of the locals in early. I haven't even connected the cask yet.'

Martin knew, above all else, how particular the locals could be about their beer. He was a nervous sort, a perennially negative soul whose glass was always half empty and even then the half left was arsenic. With his apparent discomfort with social interaction, one was forced to ponder how he'd ended up a pub landlord in the first place.

Martin changed tack quickly. 'God, Thor how are you? Sorry, you just… caught me on the hop.'

Martin had been at the meeting yesterday when Thor had almost been jackknifed quite literally into an early grave. 'I'm OK, I guess,' he replied. 'I've just come from the hospital.'

'I wasn't expecting to see you back in today, so I've got your shift tonight covered already. Is that OK? I'm sorry about that, after what happened I just assumed…'

'It's fine, Martin. Really. But if you're feeling generous, could I borrow a phone charger and a pint of cask? When it's ready of course.'

'Of course,' said Martin. 'I'm glad you're alright.' He shuffled off to locate the charger.

Thor watched him go, feeling a bit funny. He couldn't place it, but there was something about the way Martin was acting that didn't sit right. It was like he had caught him up to no good; he had explained himself very quickly, and seemed quite flustered.

It could also be the nature of our relationship, thought Thor. Martin was his boss after all, and despite him always being considerate and fair towards Thor, there was still an employee–employer relationship there. Perhaps he felt sheepish about giving Thor's shift away so hastily, without checking with Thor first?

Or maybe, Thor thought, I'm just fucking paranoid. He looked forward to that beer, as he felt it would give him calm and clarity. He was always a better pool player after he'd had one or two, maybe even three or four. How he could use such confidence and judgement today. He slumped on the bar stool.

As if to strike out any notion of not being paranoid, the back door opened with a clang, causing Thor to jump in his seat. He turned to see one of the oldest locals walk in, Pat Hurst. Despite being utterly soaked through, Pat looked like the human incarnation of an old English sheepdog, only a fraction of the size and with a flatcap balanced on his unruly grey hair. He walked almost at half speed and could barely see Thor through his wild, sodden fringe.

''Ow do, Thor. A pint please,' he said as he took off his cap and actually wrung it out with a wet dribble onto the floor of the pub.

'I'm not actually on today, Pat, but… ah, what the hell,' said Thor as he hopped from his seat and went round to the other side of the bar. 'Martin is changing the cask, but is there anything else I can get you?'

'Nay, jus' cask,' Pat replied. He had brought an odour in with him— the outdoors, dirty wet clothes, and a soupçon of poor hygiene.

Thor shrugged and started pulling a pint from the cask pump regardless. He knew better than to argue with Pat, who was a stickler when it came to his beer. As he was pulling what looked to be the grimmest pint in the pub's history, Thor remembered that Pat worked as a farmhand up on Crook's Farm.

'How are things up there today, what with the weather and all?' he asked.

"Tis teeming, and awe'm jiggered,' Pat said. His thick Lancashire accent with its quaint phrases always took a moment to decipher. In this instance, it was raining heavily and Pat was tired. 'Suff's buggered already.'

Thor had to think about that one. 'Suff's?'

'Drains, tha doowerstop.' Drains, you doorstop. Sounded like Crook's farm was in a bit of trouble with the excess water.

'And the plans? I assume they've been talking about it?' Thor put the pint on the bar.

'Plans? Dunno. By 'eck, tis flatter than Chernobyl.'

Thor frowned. Hurst didn't know anything, and he thought his pint was flatter than Chernobyl, a phrase he'd heard Pat use only a couple of hundred times before, even when the pint in question was just fine.

Still, Thor had learned the farm was in a bit of turmoil with the weather at least. It made him even more anxious to see that Roisin was alright.

Martin reappeared, greeted Pat with an ''Ow do' of his own, and handed Thor the charger.

'Thanks,' Thor said. 'Mind if I plug it in here?'

'Go for it,' Martin answered, before catching sight of Pat's desperate pint. He shook his head. 'Couldn't wait, could we Pat?' he said as he pulled the freshest looking pint of creamy ale into a new glass for Thor.

'Bugger,' muttered Pat, watching the gold flow.

Martin turned to Thor as he was plugging the charger into a socket under the bar. 'Is there anything I can do for you, Thor?'

Thor saw the earnest honesty in Martin's eyes. He felt in his gut as if he could trust him, even if he didn't know what Martin knew about things, nor what his stance on the building development might be.

'Not right now, Martin, but thanks. I've got to get a few things straight, but if I end up in a pickle, I'll let you know.'

'You and getting in a pickle is pretty much iron clad. In that case, I won't go too far.' Martin patted his shoulder as he left for the front lounge.

20

As soon as Thor had ten percent charge, he went down into the pub cellar, nestled himself between the pipes, barrels and cobwebs, and called Roisin. She answered immediately, as if camped by the phone.

'You're there!' she gasped. Thor knew immediately that she had been crying, the words spilling weak and ragged. 'Are you OK? Tell me, you are OK? They wouldn't let me see you, and I worried…'

'Roisin. I'm fine, I'm fine,' Thor interrupted. 'It's OK. Are you OK?' 'Yes, I'm fine, they just thought I was in shock, so they kept me in.'

Thor thought she still might be in shock.

'Listen, don't worry, sweetheart. The police are involved now.'

Roisin exhaled sharply. 'You told that detective? I didn't say anything.'

'I know you didn't. Thank you.'

'I'm so glad you did, though. Someone has to stop this.'

'I know. Listen, I think I know who it is. In fact, I'm sure of it. Do your family know about the building plans for Crook's Hollow?'

'You think it's to do with that?' 'I do.'

'Mum came to pick me up from the hospital. She knows, but she didn't say much. I think it's all a bit much for her. I tried to come and see you but there was a policeman on the door who wouldn't let me in.' That reassured Thor a touch, but it still didn't explain where the policeman had gone when Clyne had turned up. But Thor could well imagine Clyne stuffing a crisp fifty note into the officer's pocket and telling him to buy something from the shop downstairs for his kids.

'Look, I want for all the world to see you, but I just can't yet.' 'Why?' She sounded lost, and hurt.

'They tried to get me, and they were prepared to hurt you in the process. I can't have that happen again. I just won't. Not until I know more.'

'But I need to see you,' Roisin whispered, and Thor could hear a sob welling in her throat.

'I need to see you too. I love you, Roisin. And I don't care who knows. Nothing quite like nearly getting killed twice to bring perspective. That's why I can't risk you getting hurt, because I love you.' Thor had never said anything so honest in his life.

'I love you too,' Roisin replied, and he could hear through the shape of her words that she was smiling.

'So let's get this over with, and then let's be in love, OK?'

Thor was desperate to touch her. He ran his palm along the rough cellar wall, which crumbled whitewash flakes into the musty air.

'Yes, lets.' She let the sob that she'd had been holding in go, and it sounded wet and snotty. 'Sorry,' she said, laughing.

It sounded like sweet music to Thor. 'I'll be in touch later,' he said. 'Love you.'

'Love you, too.' Thor hung up.

He felt strong, fortified, ten feet tall and growing. He could do this. He could beat Clyne. He'd go to the police, as soon as he was certain. But that meant seeing his family and getting things straight from them, and for once in his life, he felt ready for it.

21

Loxley Farm was in uproar.

As soon as Thor arrived in the yard, and saw all the vehicles parked up on the flattened mud of the driveway, he could see it was crisis time for his family. He had got a lift from Pat, in his old pickup truck that made heavy weather of the heavy weather. As Thor jogged across the mud to the old farmhouse, he thought there must be a family meeting underway.

He jumped up on the old porch, almost losing his balance as his muddy shoes hit the soaked decking. The rain was coming down hard, in iron rivulets from the heavens, and the farmhouse stood tall against it, accepting the challenge. The house was three stories, and a jumble of styles and brick. It had been renovated many times but what remained resolute across each different shade and texture was broad bay windows across the ground floor and shuttered square windows across the top, smattered with the clinging remnants of last summer's ivy.

He had expected to be surrounded by dogs—like at Rue's house the

day before but only by many more of them—but there were none to be seen. Maybe they were scared by the ungodly weather. At the old oak door, the single remnant left untouched since the inception of the farm in 1751, he hesitated. He felt tense, foolish, and nervous.

You can choose your friends, but you can't choose your family, he thought. He set his jaw, remembered why he was here, and pushed it open.

He was in no way prepared for what he saw when he opened the door.

The front door opened onto a small raised reception area, then two steps down straight into the kitchen. But this was no kitchen anymore—it was a muddy pond filled with people.

'Close the door!' came the shout, as Thor realised he'd been standing there aghast. He didn't even know who said it.

'No, keep it open!' said someone else. 'The crap wagon will be here any minute.'

He could see his father at the centre of the furore in his shirt- sleeves, soaked. He was on his knees in eighteen inches of water, with his hands submerged. He seemed to be holding something in place, and it was only when Thor noticed the inverted wooden legs pointing to the ceiling that he saw it was the old dining table Wilkes Sr. was pushing down into the water.

'It won't stop, but it has to,' his father shouted.

Surrounding him were his brothers and his sister Mercy, each manning a table leg. Thor rushed forward to help, wading into the centre of the kitchen, through the bits and pieces that were floating on the surface.

'What's happened?' Thor shouted.

'The old well under the kitchen,' said Wilkes Jr., his eldest brother. 'It's burst through.'

Thor remembered being told as a child that in the kitchen, under the stone flags, was an old well used by their forefathers. It had long since been sealed up with the advent of running water and plumbing in the house, but the recent rainfall had obviously caused a major imbalance in the water table.

'What can I do?' Thor said, standing there while they struggled to hold the table fast. They evidently couldn't grip it in place to stem the flow, as evidenced by the swirl around their legs.

Thor had an idea. 'Is there anything else down there? Just the table?'

'Just the table, trying to hold the stone in place.' said his father, muddy water splashing into his face and hair.

'Hold on, I'll be right back,' Thor shouted as he waded out of the

kitchen by the rear door. Two steps up and he was in the downstairs hallway, which had water trickling along from where it was sloshing up over the kitchen steps. He hoped he remembered where everything was...

He ran to the stairs, spraying water up the wall, and as he turned to take the first step, he glanced into the old family room.

His mother, Bunny, was reading a story to her seven grandchildren, who were sitting on the old rug by the fire with all the dogs around them. They were huddled, wide-eyed, staring, firelight licking their cheeks, as Bunny read to them from a battered old book Thor recognised instantly.

This must have been what wartime was like, thought Thor.

Rue was there, on the sofa holding Andrew, worry creasing her brow, and she looked relieved when she caught sight of Thor in the doorway.

Immediately, he felt a surge of compassion for his family, and almost forgave them everything that instant. He couldn't stop, though, and took the stairs two at a time.

Top of the middle landing, airing cupboard on the left: it was just as he remembered. He flung it open and saw towels stacked there. Bunny always said that with six kids, living on a farm, they could never have enough clean towels. Thor grabbed as many as he could carry and ran back down the stairs.

As soon as he got in the kitchen, he put the towels on his siblings' shoulders. He got on his knees in the freezing water, and gasped.

'Jesus... Right, now lift the table and pass me towels one at a time when I put my hand out, got it?'

They looked at each other mutely, then their father took the lead. 'Got it,' he said. They pulled the table up, and Thor plunged into the water.

He felt for the crack with his fingers, following the surge that pushed his hands away like magnets of the same pole. It didn't take him long to find it but he was amazed at the powerful push of the water that was funneling through a crack about six inches wide. He came back up for air.

'Got it,' he said, reaching for a towel. His brother Hollis shoved a huge one into his hand.

'A smaller one,' said Thor.

Mercy offered a regular sized bath towel, which Thor grabbed before he submerged again. He pushed the end into the crack with effort, and jammed it until the towel was half way through. He reached out of the water, and Crewe handed him another towel.

Thor repeated the process over and over, snatching intermittent breaths, until the water pressure began to lessen. When he felt there was no more water coming through, he applied pressure to the plug of towels with his feet.

'Let's put the table back over it,' he suggested, and while they did that, he used the last remaining towel to dry himself with futility. Calm slowly returned to the room, and the family stood back and regarded him. Now that the urgency of the moment had receded, the feeling of distrust returned.

'What are you doing here?' asked Crewe. His eyes were filled with a diluted distaste.

'I came to speak to you all,' Thor said. 'But I'd like to speak with Dad first.'

Wilkes Sr. looked up, more surprised at Thor calling him Dad than anything else.

'He's a traitor, Dad,' said Mercy, her stout features set like a granite, albeit fatter, Easter Island head. 'He's not one of us anymore.'

Wilkes Sr. glanced at her, then leaned back against the sink. 'Yes, but he may just have saved the farm. Well, the farmhouse at least. I'll hear him out.' He turned to Thor. 'Let's speak in private.'

'Dad,' Mercy said, letting her jaw hang low, revealing her teeth to be yellowed and wayward. 'He'd see us all in the street.'

Thor just looked at her, resigned. He knew they probably all felt this way, and there was nothing he could do about it; but it stung to hear such feelings given voice.

'Yes, Mercy, we all know what you think on this particular topic. In fact, we tend to know what you think about most topics.' Wilkes Sr. started towards the hallway. 'Let's go to the office, Thornton. And you lot watch out for the crap wagon, alright?'

Wilkes Sr.'s children looked at him with surprise, and they looked to each other for guidance. Bunch of sheep, thought Thor, as he trudged up and out of the kitchen in his father's watery wake.

The first door on the left in the hallway led to the farmhouse office. It was a shoebox clad in old wood and horse-brasses, featuring a desk, a couple of chairs, and an old scratched metal filing cabinet. The Loxleys were outdoor people and always had been, and there was little use for a grand office. The accounts were stored in the attic, so it was just the day-to-day running of things that was taken care of in here. No pictures adorned the walls, save for a birds-eye view of the farm from the air. Thor remembered

164

the day it arrived. Some chancer knocked on the door with the photograph all framed up, with the story that he had flown over the whole area taking pictures, and was selling prints to those that wanted them. Young Thor thought there would be no remote chance of his hardline father agreeing to buy something from a hawker on the door. But he had surprised Thor then, just as he was surprising him today.

Their shoes squelched on the stone tiles, leaving patches of off- brown water. The clean-up was already set to be huge, but there was nowhere else appropriate for a quiet moment. Wilkes Sr. stepped towards the other side of the desk and stood with his back to Thor, as if he were readying himself. Still facing the wall, he growled, 'I'm glad you are alright. After the accident yesterday, I mean.'

It was the first time any of Thor's family had acknowledged what had happened. Not knowing what else to do, Thor simply nodded.

'I owe Ma a new headstone. How did you find out about it?' Thor asked, standing awkwardly by the door.

'Martin Campbell called straight away. He's a good bloke - said you were OK. He said he'd go to the hospital with you.'

Thor was surprised to hear that, and grateful. His boss had taken him to the hospital but hadn't even mentioned it to Thor.

'Not you, though?' Thor said, trying to keep it light but aware his words were stern.

'I didn't think you'd like that,' Wilkes Sr. said after a moment. 'Your mother and I... didn't want to upset you. And Martin promised that you were OK.'

'It was an attempt on my life,' Thor said.

'You're sure?' Wilkes Sr. still hadn't turned around, and a steady

drip drip had started on the edge of the desk from his arm.

'Well, the detective who interviewed me seemed to think as much... I'm supposed to be in hospital, with a police guard, but I couldn't stay there. Left a couple of hours ago.'

Wilkes Sr. finally turned and eyed his son with a look that Thor hadn't seen in eons: a caring look. 'Why the bloody hell did you do that?' he asked.

'Because it was the second time someone had tried it. The first happened the night before.'

That seemed to shake Wilkes Sr., who looked to the floor as if searching his memory, then finding it. 'At church... your questions?'

'Yes.' Thor looked hard at his father, silently imploring him to tell the truth.

'Thornton, you daft bastard, we've had our differences, but if you know anything about the Loxleys, we are fiercely loyal. We would never harm our own blood. Never.'

The old man looked deeply offended. 'Try telling that to Mercy.'

Wilkes Sr.'s voice took on a fervour. 'You turned your back on all of us, Thornton. All the generations of Loxleys since passed, you threw it back in all their faces. Is there any wonder your brothers and sisters, who have always done things the right way, might feel anger towards you?'

Thor knew this line well. If he didn't steer it back, it would end up just like the argument that saw him walking out of the house for good a couple of years ago. Before he could speak, a soft clicking on the floor brought a battered old dog from behind the desk, yawning and investigating what had woken him.

It was Ruby, a dachshund-rottweiler freak of breeding, a loveable oddity. He was a male dog with a girl's name and he liked to sleep in there, so much so, and so often, that everyone tended to forget about him. When Thor still lived on the farm they were always having to let him back out, scratching at the door in the morning, so he could join the other dogs at the embers of the previous night's hearth.

'What's done is done,' Thor said. 'I want to know who has been trying to kill me, and I'm pretty sure I know who it is. I need to cross a few names off first.'

'I don't need to tell you it was no one here, do I? Don't make me suffer the indignity of having to say it.'

'But… the parish hall meeting yesterday. I can't believe you weren't there. It could change everything for everyone.'

Wilkes turned to the desk, cracked open the top drawer, and rummaged inside. 'We didn't need to go.'

'Why not?'

Wilkes pulled out a folder.

'Because we'd already been told of the plans.'

Wilkes tossed the folder to Thor, who thumbed it open quickly. It was a copy of what appeared to be the entire COMUDEV proposal.

'They wanted to get us onside.'

'How long have you known?' Thor asked, gobsmacked. 'A few days.'

'Were you going to tell me?'

Wilkes sat on the edge of the desk and heaved a sigh. 'You've made your feelings quite clear a number of times. Your affairs and ours separated the minute you turned your back on the Loxley tradition with your piece of land. And we all know which piece of land that Clyne bastard needs from us—yours.'

'So why did he come to see you? If it's my land, not yours, he needs?'

Wilkes grimaced. 'He was a cocky shite. A real city slicker. He knew what we'd think about such an idea and he knew we couldn't do anything about it. I think he wanted to come here to try to get a feel for what you might say to any kind of offer, and to really rub our noses in it.'

A few things begin to pull into focus for Thor.

'He knew we'd had a falling-out,' said Thor. 'He knew our interests

might not be the same. He picked the weakest point in the family armour.'

Wilkes Sr. nodded. 'His local knowledge is sound, you have to give him that. He needed a bit more land, and he knew you were the most likely route to it.'

Thor thought back to what Mercy had said in the kitchen. He'll see us out in the street. It suddenly made sense.

'But what about the Crooks?' Thor said. 'So much more of their land is needed for Clyne's plan…'

'According to Clyne, they have agreed to sell what he wants.

According to Clyne, when they do it's going to make them rich.'

Thor felt punched in the gut. Thor's land, it appeared, was the only thing stopping them from helping Clyne realise his dream, if the Crooks were already onside. And that brought the whole Crook family's motives into question. Even Roisin would benefit.

Something that'll really piss your dad off. That's what Wendell had said about what they'd been doing the night Thor was attacked in the field.

'Jesus,' muttered Thor.

'Bloody Brexit did for us,' said Wilkes Sr., referring to the EU referendum Great Britain had voted on earlier in the year, which saw a narrow victory for the Leave campaign jettison the country from the economic safety of the European Union. 'We were heavily subsidised by the Common Agriculture Policy, but when we voted out, the instability rocked the entire agriculture sector. Our farms, what we produce: it's all worth a lot less now.'

Thor, in his bubble away from the farm, hadn't remotely considered the impact Brexit would have on the family. It made the Crooks' acceptance of the deal a lot easier to understand.

The Crooks suddenly loomed large as another party that would be well served by Thor's death, ready to make the Crooks a fortune. Thor felt a cold sweat breaking between his shoulder blades.

'What did you think I was going to do?' Thor asked.

'We didn't know. Honestly. We were scared that the fall-out between us was so irreparable that you would let Clyne have the land he wanted, and it would put us out of business.'

'Out of business?' Thor was perplexed. 'Why would it put you out of business?'

Wilkes Sr. walked to the aerial photograph and pointed to the outlying fields, on the edge of the property. 'When plans like these are made, nobody considers the impact on the adjacent land. The water in the kitchen, that's groundwater. Nobody apart from those who have worked this land know that Crook's Hollow sits on a groundwater deluge. The earth is just utterly sodden beneath is. This extra rain has flooded the very underground, and the well was the first thing to buckle under the strain.'

'Oh my God.'

'And all the fields Clyne wants to build on, that the council has apparently agreed to let him build on, are vital to the water table and the drainage of this area. You fill that land with concrete, pipes, and roadways, and take away all that natural drainage, you have a problem. That water, that deluge beneath us, has to go

172

somewhere, and the only place it can go is out onto our land.'

The reality of it hit Thor like a hammer-strike. 'We'd be flooded out of business.'

'Nine months of the year, two thirds of the farm would be underwater. We'd have to leave.'

Thor had never thought about any such thing, that building homes could have such a disastrous impact on the outlying area. And it wasn't as if Clyne or the Crooks would give a rat's arse if it put the Loxley family out of business.

Thor reached in his pocket and pulled out the cheque Clyne gave him. He held it out for Wilkes Sr. to see, but Wilkes Sr. had to put his glasses on first. Instead of opening them fully, he just held them to his eyes. His jaw lowered, as he looked at Thor.

A million things must have been going through Wilkes Sr.'s mind, but Thor did what he least expected: he tore the cheque into small pieces, and threw the scraps to the floor.

'This is family,' Thor said. 'My family won't be on the street, even if we don't agree on everything.'

Wilkes's eyes filled with a mixture of relief, shock, and love, as he put a hand on Thor's shoulder. It was a look Thor would never forget.

'Thank you, son,' he said.

'Crap wagon's here!' shouted someone from the kitchen.

'Come on,' said Thor, leading the way back into the huge indoor pond where they used to break bread.

As they entered, his siblings were helping haul a huge hose into the kitchen, leaving the remainder snaking out of the front door. Thor finally understood why the crap wagon was here. Primarily used for emptying septic tanks, it was essentially a big water tank on wheels that could suck the contents of the kitchen into its belly, and drain the kitchen. It would take time, and leave a real mess, but after a few trips it would get it done.

And then Thor saw the driver of the wagon. The wagon driver was Jason Dwyer, his old school friend.

Thor had forgotten he'd taken over the business from his father last year. Jason, in his tattered grey overalls and bright yellow wellies, caught his eye, and nodded to him coldly.

And in his left hand, held up next to his chin, rested an e-cigarette vaporiser, connected to a small bright blue cartridge—exactly like the one left in the field the night Thor had nearly been killed.

22

Thor stood on the step watching the water slowly inch lower. It left a mucky residue up the kitchen cabinets, and a bad smell of river water, pollution, and compost. He watched Jason, hoping that some look of uncertainty or guilt would reveal to Thor the acknowledgement of the awkwardness a would-be killer might feel when his prey just won't die.

But Thor could detect nothing.

His siblings watched Thor with challenging eyes, almost daring him to stand up to them, while the flood water gurgled up the tube. Thor felt good to know that, despite their obvious animosity, on this occasion he had done the right thing. He was sure his father would fill them in at some point.

During the stifling awkwardness in the kitchen, an arm came up behind Thor and linked through his own.

'I'm so glad to see you,' said Rue, resting her head on Thor's shoulder. 'When I heard what happened yesterday, after what we had just talked about, I could only assume the worst.'

'I'm fine,' said Thor. 'Don't worry. We are getting to the bottom of it.' He couldn't take his eyes off Jason, who sucked on that e-cigarette like it was the dregs of a ninety-nine with sprinkles.

'Mum and Dad got the call from the hospital, then let us all know. They said you were fine. I'd have been there in a heartbeat if it wasn't for the kids. Barry's doing triple shifts on the roads, and the weather's sent everything sideways.'

'Don't worry, sis. The police are involved now.'

'I'd imagined they'd have to be, with you ending up in hospital and
everything.'

'Yeah, between them and me, we'll get this sorted.'

Rue squeezed his arm. 'Leave it to them. Please, Thor. That's twice we've nearly lost you. I'm worried sick.'

Suddenly, Jason started pulling the tube back out of the water, even though there was still six inches of water on the floor. 'I've got to go dump this lot,' he said. 'I'll come back for the rest.'

'Just not anywhere on the farm, please, Jason,' said Wilkes Sr. 'You don't want me to just spray it on the field?'

'Of course not, you idiot,' said Hollis. 'The brook over at the end of Hob Lane, you could dump it in that.'

'You think?' Jason didn't look too thrilled with that idea, nor having just been called an idiot.

'I'll go with you,' said Thor, before he even knew he was planning on saying anything at all. Jason looked at him with arched eyebrows. 'I'll give you a hand, then you can drop me off in the Hollow.'

He actually wanted a ride to Crook's Farm, but there was no way he was going to say that in front of this lot.

'Sounds a great idea,' said Mercy, as she stepped up into the hall. Thor knew exactly which bit of the idea she thought was great—the bit with him leaving.

'Alright,' said Jason begrudgingly. 'I'll just load up the hose, then we can get going'.

'I'll wait in the cab,' Thor said. He gave Rue a goodbye hug, and a goodbye nod to his father. He didn't know what else to do, but he certainly saw his dad in a different light now. Maybe Rue was right after all, he thought. Loyalty did seem to count for something.

As Thor walked across the kitchen, getting his shoes sodden all over again, he was forced to acknowledge that, through all that had happened, neither himself nor his father had covered themselves in glory. Wilkes Sr. should have been gentler with his son regarding his wishes, and more understanding of the situation. Thor himself perhaps should have been less reactionary and petulant. Either way, Thor felt for the first time that things might just be saved between himself and his family.

He ran across the yard to the crap wagon, the rain driving harder than ever. It was getting to feel like an eerie precursor to the apocalypse, with the moody gloom so thick you couldn't even glance up to get a look at it.

He jumped up into the cab, scooting Lucozade bottles and copies of The Daily Star off the seat and into the muddy footwell. In the wing mirror, he could see Jason attaching the hose to the back of the truck, and he tried to get his line of questioning in order. He had to make it look innocent, but that was hard when he thought of what he was now contemplating: that Jason Dwyer had been cajoled by Clyne and the Crooks to kill him, and given Thor and Jason's up-and-down past, Jason had been only too happy to do it for them.

With a burst of crashing water, Jason opened the door and was in the cab with him.

'What a fucking day,' he said, partly to Thor but mainly to whatever god he might believe in.

'Never seen anything like it,' conceded Thor.

'I tell you what, Thor, you've got some big bollocks asking for a ride into the Hollow from me,' said Jason, as he started the truck and flicked the wipers on. They made little difference, just moved sheets of water from one side to the other.

'You didn't expect me to walk in this, did you?' Thor attempted to jokc, but it fell flat. There was too much history between them and too much at stake. He decided to play it softly. 'Look, I'm sorry for coming to see you at home like that yesterday.'

Jason didn't say anything as he carefully pushed through the mud of the driveway, guiding his wagon through the bog. Thor pressed on.

'I was scared. It was a bad one. Whoever did it tried to run me over with a combine harvester.' If Thor was expecting some kind of reveal from Jason, he wasn't getting one; his features were a mask of passive concentration. 'Either way, I shouldn't have come to your house like that, pointing fingers. For that I'm sorry.'

'Do you know where this brook is?' Jason said, his eyes glued to the road ahead.

'Yeah.'

'Then you can direct me. I'll head to Hob, and you can tell me where.'

By glossing over Thor's attempt at opening up a line of communication, Jason had taken the wind out of Thor's sails. They sat in silence for a moment, as Jason wound the truck off the smaller country lanes onto the main road leading to Crook's Hollow.

Thor remembered where he wanted to go, and who he thought Jason's co-conspirators were. 'After we've dumped the load, can you drop me off at Crook's

182

Farm instead? Actually at the end of Crook's Hollow itself?'

Jason turned and glanced at Thor—a look that broke into a very small smile.

'What?' Thor asked, feeling the hairs on his neck rise arrow- straight.

'So it's true,' said Jason, his eyes back on the rain-spattered windshield.

'What is?'

'You and the youngest Crook girl,' he said. 'What's her name again?' 'Roisin.'

'I'd never've thought it possible. A Loxley and a Crook.'

There was a bite in Jason's words, an ill-disguised tone of distaste. 'You know them, don't you?' Thor said, trying to take back control

of the conversation. 'The Crooks?'

'Only in the way everyone knows them. Distant big-wigs who don't mix with the small and less important. They think they know everything.'

Again, there was the bite that Thor couldn't decipher. Jason obviously had his own thoughts, his own feelings, his own concerns and judgements.

As the wagon entered onto the main street of Crook's Hollow, imaginatively called Main Street, they passed the village primary school. A low, grey-brick building that was built in the late sixties to accommodate the rush of kids being born on the then-new estate.

'Do you ever wish we were still there?' Jason asked, nodding towards the school. In the grey murk of the day, all the lights were on inside.

'Always. Happiest times of my life,' Thor replied. 'And the simplest.'

They left the school behind and drove past the post office.

'How is it up there?' asked Jason. He seemed to have lost a little of the bile that had flavoured his earlier words.

'It's not the Savoy or anything, but it works. Nice to have my own space. It was madness growing up on the farm. That place is the first thing I ever had that wasn't a hand-me-down.'

Jason laughed. 'Yeah, I remember you in your sister's jeans. One pair even had stitched fairy wings around the pockets—didn't we colour them in with a marker pen to look like Batman?'

Thor could only smile at this very fond memory.

'I got in so much trouble, but those pants went from the worst jeans I'd ever had to my favourite.'

'Simpler times,' Jason said again.

Thor felt a pang of empathy for his old friend. A gulf of different lifestyle choices and family circumstances separated them, but deep down there was a lot that bonded them, and with every passing moment Thor found it harder to believe his old friend would try to kill him.

'Take this left,' Thor said. As Jason turned the wheel, Thor said, 'So how long have you been vaping?' He tried to make it sound casual.

'A couple of weeks. Trying to kick the main habit, you know. And those other ones you don't approve of, believe it or not.'

'The cartridges expensive?' Thor thought of the one in his pocket. 'Nah, not really. A few quid here and there. Better than cigs either

way.'

'You ever lose one?'

The oddness of the question wasn't lost on Jason. He glanced over at Thor. 'What do you mean, lose one?'

'I found one—oh shit, stop here.'

As they came to the end of Hob Lane, the brook rose before them. Usually no more than a small creek running down a shallow embankment, it was now spurting white water up onto the road. As Jason pulled the wagon up, Thor could see the brook had completely overflowed its banks and was running wildly. His father had been right about the fragility of the water table here—the weather was wreaking havoc with it.

'I've never seen that before,' Thor said.

'What do you mean you found one?' pressed Jason, clearly not having forgotten Thor's change of direction moments earlier.

'I have it here,' Thor said, pulling out the cartridge. He held it next to the e-cig that Jason had put on the dashboard. The cartridges were identical.

'What do you know—a match.'

Thor looked at Jason, who looked back. 'What the fuck do you mean, Thor?'

'Want to guess where I got this one?' 'Not really, no.'

'Whoever tried to kill me on Saturday night dropped it. I got it from the field.'

Jason sat gaping. Then he laughed, a dark, cruel cackle. 'You pathetic little shit. Get out.'

Thor sat solid where he was. 'Was it you?' 'You stupid fucking moron, look around you.'

'I'm just asking you, tell me straight—was it you?'

'I tell you what, Thor,' Jason said, and he jumped out of the cab. He walked round the front to the passenger side and pulled the door open. 'Get the fuck out.'

Jason grabbed Thor by the jacket and yanked him bodily out of the wagon.

Thor fought back, scrambled for his balance, and pushed Jason off him.

'Fuck off,' Jason shouted. 'I mean it, if you know what's good for you, you'll fuck off right now.'

'Did you do it, Jason?' Thor shouted over the deluge, but Jason was walking to the rear of the wagon. 'Did you do it?'

Jason reappeared with the hose, and with a flick of the valve, water sprayed forth from the hose, hitting Thor like a battering ram. He was

swept off his feet and sent tumbling onto the asphalt. Jason kept directing the water at him, and the sheer volume of it pushed him ever closer to the raging water of the brook.

Thor suddenly felt panic at the thought of tumbling in, being washed down and away with the torrent. He held on to the road, gripping the asphalt as best he could, digging his fingers into whatever crevices they could find, as the contents of his parents' kitchen was emptied onto him.

It felt like being stuck under a wave that would not stop crashing on his head, an interminable wipeout. Nor could he forget the fact that the water being dumped on him had been stored in the crap wagon, essentially a bacteria factory on wheels.

The pressure began to dwindle ever so slightly, and the thunder across his back and shoulders began to lessen, then to level off. It took a moment of gasping for air for him to realise that what he now felt was simply rain.

He heard the wagon shift into gear, and the engine roared as Jason drove away, leaving him on the grass verge like a drowned scuff of roadkill.

He lay there, listening to the drum of the rain all around him, the drops peppering him. It was a bizarre sensation, one that, if it weren't for the cold, wasn't entirely unpleasant. But a wave of exhaustion hit him hard, in his weak and worn-out state. He had barely slept in two days, been beaten then battered, and survived death twice. So he just lay there.

After a moment, the growl of another engine weaved through the sound of rainfall, followed by the squeak of brakes. Thor was so done in, he just lay on his back and waited for whoever it was to get on with whatever it was they intended to do.

'Bloody hell, Thor,' said a voice he recognised. 'What are you doing out here?'

Thor felt like laughing because it was a great question. But instead he just smiled and said: 'Getting wet, by the looks of things.'

'Oh I see,' said Ahmed, the youngest of the brothers from the post office, not seeing at all. 'Well, let's get you home. You just can't stop getting into trouble can you?' Ahmed linked his arms under Thor's armpits and hoisted him up.

'You heard?' Thor replied, allowing Ahmed to help him back to Ahmed's car, a small hatchback.

'The police were round today looking for you.' Ahmed bundled him into the passenger seat then ran around the bonnet to jump in the driver's side. He immediately turned the fans on full heat, as condensation fogged the windscreen, and ran a hand through his hair, shaking off the excess water. He was in his late thirties, with a close- cropped beard and amber eyes. He looked at Thor with concern.

'What did you tell them?'

'What could I tell them? I didn't know where you were! I had to let them in your flat, though. We were worried about you, especially after yesterday at the church.'

'The village is going to shit, Ahmed. And those building plans will definitely make sure of it.'

Ahmed looked troubled. He put the car in gear and they pulled away. 'I must admit, it came as a bit of a surprise.' His accent over the years had softened. What had once been a prim, well-spoken Indian lilt now had the odd layer of broad northern England about it.

'It'll be good for business though, won't it?' Thor said, suddenly utterly fed up with the whole damn affair, but immediately regretted it. Ahmed had only ever been good to Thor, and didn't deserve such a sniping remark. Ahmed kept cool and replied with admirable frankness.

'If we managed to be the only post office here, then yes, of course it would. But those people from COMUDEV don't represent me, Thor. This community has been very good to me and my brother, even though it was hard at first. Our first position is loyalty to the Hollow, and if what those businessmen propose is bad for the Hollow, then we don't support it. Simple as.'

Thor admired his honesty, and respected his loyalty. Ahmed's integrity was obviously much deeper than Thor gave him credit for.

'I'm sorry Ahmed, I didn't intend…'

'It's alright, but already a lot of people are looking at us like that.

I've had to explain our position a few times, and it hasn't even been twenty-four hours since the plans were made public.'

Ahmed turned onto Main Street and took the left to the post office. 'I wish people realised that not every businessman is the same as

every other,' Ahmed said, with obvious sadness.

'I'm sorry, mate, I didn't mean it to come out like that.'

The car pulled in at the post office, and Ahmed swung it round the back to the car park, and the stairs to Thor's flat.

'Ah, it's alright, Thor. This must be hard for you too. I saw where they want to build, and I understand how it will affect your family.'

Thor didn't want to correct him by swapping the word affect to

devastate.

'Have you seen them?' Ahmed asked. 'Yes, I have.'

'Good. Family is everything. We send money home all the time to our family, but so much time has passed now that most of the family we send money to, we don't even know. But it's still important. We let you stay here in the hope that one day you'd make it back to yours.'

'Thanks Ahmed. I really appreciate it.'

'Go on. Get cleaned up. And I saw that leak in your bedroom radiator—I'll have someone come and take a look at it.'

All Thor could do was smile with gratitude, before easing up out of the car to clamber up the steps. The cold iced through him again after the heat of the car, slowing his climb.

When he got to the top and opened the door, he saw two things, only one of them benign.

The first was a note lying on his tattered door mat. It was from DCI Okpara. Assume you discharged yourself. I have some background information that might help. Call me ASAP. A mobile number followed.

Second—his flat had been ransacked. Every drawer, box, container, even down to the Tupperware in his tiny kitchen had been upended and emptied. Someone had been here, probably some time between the police's visit and Thor's returning home. Someone

who obviously knew where he lived, and was looking
for something

23

Any hopes of a relaxing bath and a nap—or an honest-to-God real sleep—were off the table, and Thor had to face ever more compelling realities. The person who was after him wasn't done yet, nor were they scared of the police. Every time he felt he had turned a corner, the tide swung again and he was under siege. And his escapes were getting ever narrower.

In the bathroom he stripped, adding his clothes to the smelly bin bag by the sink. He took out what he was carrying, which amounted to a soaked wallet, his keys, and a water-logged, broken phone. He must have dropped the vape cartridge in the wagon cab, or into the bursting brook, and cursed his luck. That might have been a valuable piece of evidence, now gone.

He showered, got dressed, and picked up Okpara's note. He had no landline to ring him on, but would have to get in touch with him soon, if only to report the break-in. Glancing around his flat, he surveyed the wreckage that once comprised his belongings. He tried to think if there was anything of any value that he might have kept here, but could think of nothing that would point him to what his visitor was looking for.

He felt less sure with every minute, and his thoughts ebbed to Jason. Jason's attack on Thor could have been the result of many things. It could have been a message to Thor to back off. It could simply have been one of anger at being accused yet again by Thor, just when they seemed to be sorting things out.

But the available evidence still pointed to Jason being involved in the initial attack. His theory that Jason was the puppet on strings, controlled by a bigger party, still held a degree of weight, and that pointed two ways. Clyne, and the Crooks.

And in that, somewhere, was Roisin, who said she knew nothing about the development, which would seem to preclude her knowing about any plots to kill Thor. But he didn't know enough about her relationship with her brothers and parents, what they shared and what they didn't.

But Thor believed her. She said she knew nothing, and he was not inclined to second-guess her now. He felt safe nowhere, but he had to get Roisin's thoughts on things. On whether she felt her family was capable of such a thing. On whether she could see her family accepting Clyne's proposition. Plus, he could use her phone to call Okpara, and find out what he now knew.

He'd have to head straight into the vipers' nest. Crook's Farm seemed to be the only place he would get answers.

He left his flat, this time grabbing an old golf umbrella he had been given by one of the regulars in the pub; not a local, but a tourist who had stuck around long enough to challenge the convention.

He went around to the front of the post office and entered. The office was busy in a weird way: half of it was empty, the other half had a queue containing nine or ten people. There were two cashier points, and the queue was all at one. Thor couldn't understand it, but behind the empty desk sat Mo. He looked just the same as his brother, except that his hair was that bit longer, his beard that much shorter, as if Ahmed was just that bit more precise in his appearance.

Thor beckoned him over with a discreet gesture, and Mo came from behind the cashier's glass and met Thor at the door.

'Good to see you're OK,' he said with a smile. 'I didn't fancy chasing up a dead man for rent.'

'Thanks. What's going on here?' Thor asked.

Mo spoke quietly. 'They are all queuing up to put money on their electricity meters. This weather's got them thinking the end of the world is nigh, but they don't seem to see that if the power lines go down because of a flood, we are all buggered for leccy, regardless of how much cash they've put in the meter.'

Thor nodded. 'Look, I know this is a bad time, but any chance of a ride up to Crook's Farm?'

Mo turned and looked—Ahmed was swamped.

'His till's the only one that you can do the electricity accounts from.' He turned back to Thor with a mischievous glint in his eyes. 'He'll be fine for five minutes.'

24

If there was a sun up there, high above the greys of the bulging clouds, it would have been starting its gradual tilt to the western horizon. All it meant in Crook's Hollow was that the darkness got darker. Soon, it would be nightfall.

Mo had dropped Thor off at his car, had asked no questions, and then turned back. Thor gave his car the once over, saw that everything was as it should be and that it hadn't floated off, and made the walk to the Hollow under his umbrella. The sheep were nowhere to be seen, and as Thor approached the dip in the land that signaled the start of the Hollow, he could see why.

It was flooded, and the water was moving steadily downhill to fill the woodland at the bottom. It must have been two or three inches deep, and tufts of longer grass the sheep hadn't yet reached were poking up through the surface.

Thor had to take the more difficult higher route along the drystone wall, some thirty feet above the Hollow floor. As he got to higher ground, he saw that the water continued to flow along the floor of the shallow vale, right up to where the Hollow bent right slightly— and he could see no more.

Higher up the rise, he saw the lights on in Roisin's caravan, and the sight warmed him. He hadn't seen her since he shoved her out of danger in the churchyard, and their respective trips to the hospital had been and gone. There had been so much happening, and time had flown, but he needed her now.

When he knocked on the flimsy door, he heard footsteps as she crossed the floor, then the door creaked open just enough for her to peek out. When she saw Thor, she threw the door wide and pulled him in.

'Thor!' she cried. She showered him in kisses, but in his abrupt entry his umbrella had got snagged in the door. He let go of it, and it tumbled away outside. He pulled the door closed and kissed her hard.

'You saved me,' she gasped, 'in the graveyard you saved me.'

The living room was warm. Roisin's small TV was showing Granada Tonight, the local news bulletins. A variety of throws had been used to cover the threadbare old upholstery, with different colours and cushions, giving the impression of the world's smallest Moroccan boudoir. A votive candle burned on the side table, and a mug of tea steamed next to it.

Roisin was wearing an old university hoodie and fleece lounge pants, with thick striped walking socks. Her hair was up in a lazy bun, with stray strands snaking down her neck. She wore glasses, as she always did when she watched television. It was a look that Thor thought nobody else in the world could pull off but her—let alone carry off as smouldering. And yet here Roisin was doing it, and at a canter, too.

If he could have married her there and then, he would have.

They kissed, as they fell onto the sofa, and Thor felt all his fears and concerns about Roisin's family fall to the back of his mind. His hands found their way into the back of her hoodie, and gripped her warm, soft hips.

'I love you,' she said.

'I love you, too,' he whispered, and it felt like the most natural, right, correct thing in the world.

They wound further into each other, the tensions of the last day unravelling. Desire soon caught up with them both, and when it could be held back no more, they turned the lights off but left the candle burning. The rain drummed an urgent beat on the roof, masking the sounds of all else.

A couple of moments later, Thor's mind seemed to get stuck changing gears. He felt there would be time for this later, but he had so much he wanted to ask, to check on, to get out. Roisin sensed his engine stall.

'Are you OK?' she asked.

'I'm fine. There's so much to talk about, and... I can't concentrate.

I'm sorry.'

'That's OK. It's been a mad couple of days. Shall we have a cup of tea and a snuggle? Talk for a while?'

Thor couldn't have wished for anything better.

'We've got plenty of time—and you are staying here tonight with me. There's no discussion there.'

Thor nodded and smiled.

'Let me make them,' he said, and hopped up. He went into the adjoining kitchenette and boiled the kettle. 'My head is just fried, there's so much going on.'

'I know,' said Roisin, pulling a blanket around her. 'The Hollow just got so much weirder.'

'We never got a chance to talk about it, before…' He squeezed the tea bag against the side of the mug with a teaspoon—a technique Ma Loxley would have hated, bless her soul. She was a teapot lady through and through, a characteristic Rue now carried.

'The plans, you mean? I know. They would change everything around here.'

She plucked nervously at the frayed edges of the blankct she was swaddled in. Thor felt there was more she wanted to share, but didn't want to push her. But still, he needed to know what she knew.

'I went to my parents',' he said, bringing the mugs over.

'You did?' exclaimed Roisin, as she took a tea, scalding herself slightly as it sloshed over the sides.

'You OK?'

'Yeah.' She swapped the mug to her other hand and sucked her finger. Her nerves seemed to be bubbling, but she was gamely doing her best to stay strong in the face of everything. 'How did it go? I wish I could have been there with you. Would like to have helped.'

'Thanks, but it was OK. Really, they had way more on their minds than any old trouble with me. The kitchen was flooded.'

'Flooded? How?'

'The well had given in.' Thor looked away from her for a second, trying to organise how to bring up the next part. 'The plans affect both our families, right? And their land—you saw that on the map.'

Roisin straightened. 'How could I miss it?'

'When I saw my family… they said your family had agreed to it.

That they had agreed to sell Clyne what he needed.'

Roisin stared into her tea like the answers were stored in its depths.

Her bottom lip began to quiver.

'Sweetheart,' Thor said, 'I know this is weird for us, but we need to talk about it. Please. Do you know what your family are going to do?'

Tears started to roll from under her glasses, but she didn't give in to sobbing.

'They made the decision without me. I had nothing to do with it. Thor, you must believe me, I didn't know until I saw the plans yesterday, and I certainly didn't know they were going to go along with it until Mum picked me up from the hospital this morning.'

'So they are going through with it?' Thor sat close, facing her, but she still wouldn't look up.

'That's what Mum says, but I'm still not ready to believe it. It's huge pieces of the farm, gone.'

Thor asked the big question. 'Who owns the land— the land that Clyne wants to buy?'

'Mum and Dad,' she replied, but she looked up hurt. 'I won't be getting any of it, don't worry about me doing better because of it. I won't see any of that money.'

Thor placed a hand on her knee. 'Hey, I didn't mean that. I just want to know what we are dealing with, that's all.'

Roisin's voice began to quiver. 'I'll have to leave. They'll pack up the farm because they'll have made all they'll ever need to. I'll be left with nothing and nowhere to go.'

'No, you won't, I'd never let that happen.' Thor shifted around to sit behind her, and she lay back against his chest. He spoke softly. 'The same thing will happen to me.'

'What do you mean? They only need a little bit from your family,

don't they?' She wiped her tears away with a sleeve.

'If they build where they say they are going to, the natural drainage of the land will be changed for the worse. My family's farm would be flooded. You, me, they—we'd lose everything together.'

'Oh my God,' whispered Roisin.

This was stick or twist time for Thor, the moment when he could reveal his hand. He just didn't know which way it was going to go. His land, and his ownership of it, held the key to it all, and could decide the fortunes of both their families, in different ways. If he were to sell, he'd condemn his own family's farm. If he refused to sell, Roisin's family would miss out on the deal of a lifetime, assuming Clyne had made them an offer relative to the one he made to Thor.

Roisin beat him to it. 'We have to stop them,' she said.

It was a good job, Thor thought, considering he had already ripped up the cheque.

'What can we do?'

'I think I've already done it,' said Thor. 'What do you mean?'

Roisin was wide eyed how Thor explained that the piece of land Clyne needed was a land gift from his parents, that it belonged to him. She was dumbfounded when he told her about Clyne's offer and the cheque, which was now in scraps.

Thor had come clean about the land, the reason for the family falling-out, the reason for his outcast state, and it felt amazing.

'I think as far as the development is concerned, it'll be OK,' he finished. 'As long as the police catch who has been trying to kill me and I can stay alive long enough to stop the development going forward.'

'You wonderful, brave man,' said Roisin, as she clambered onto him, kissing him. 'I love you.'

This time, no talk came between them. Thor didn't stall. The candlelight was all the light they needed.

25

He was awakened at just gone twelve by Roisin shaking him. She was silent when she did it, and somehow that told him to remain quiet too. As his eyes focused in the gloom, he was met with hers: urgent and insistent. She mouthed something, he shook his head, and she tried again. This time she used just a little breath, so the words were no more than scratched air.

'Someone is in here.'

He hopped up immediately, wearing just his boxer shorts, and Roisin tangled on a t-shirt. He crouched by the door, listening.

Nothing.

All he noticed was that the rain was softer. Roisin joined him on the floor, poised, cat-like. They listened.

The softest thud could be heard from the lounge. They looked at each other as if to ask, Did you hear it too?

It came again, an almost imperceptible sound, but it was all the proof they needed. Roisin was right.

Someone was in the caravan with them.

Thor realised his error—being here with Roisin and no one knowing where he was—but as soon as the thoughts surfaced he smothered them immediately with a more urgent idea, namely survival, for the pair of them. A third attempt on his life would surely leave nothing to chance.

He glanced around the room, checking for anything they could use to defend themselves.

The thud again. Closer. Heading for the bedroom.

'Get under the bed,' Thor whispered to Roisin, but she shook her head. She picked up the lamp from her bedside table; it was nothing more than a small wooden block with an Edison bulb embedded in its surface. Thor had always liked it, and thought that in a pinch it would at least slow down their attacker. The room was so tiny that Thor couldn't think of what else to use, save for a coat hanger, some books, and a string of flimsy fairy lights. His hands would have to do.

Thor focused on the door, and held his breath.

Thud, again. Just by the door. Whoever it was, had stopped just beyond the door. A squeak of the flooring suggested a shifting of weight, and in the darkness, Thor could just make out the door sagging very slightly under the weight of their visitor.

Whoever it was was leaning against the door, listening.

Thor threw himself at the door, shoulder first, putting every ounce of his weight behind it, an explosion of movement that caused Roisin to gasp.

The door buckled and its hinges gave way. The intruder's weight was on the other side, but unbalanced, and Thor dug in and pushed as hard as he could, forcing the intruder to stagger back. As Thor shoved harder, his adversary seemed to trip, and Thor fell forward onto the door.

They crashed to the floor, the door sandwiched between them.

Thor hadn't yet seen the intruder's face. 'Call the police, Roisin!' he shouted.

'Thor!' she shouted back, just behind him, but he heard nothing else as his skull felt crushed by a dense impact.

His last thought before the blackness came for him again was his certainty that there was not one but two intruders, and that he could do nothing to stop them from harming Roisin.

26

It wasn't raining any more.

It was windy, but at least it wasn't pissing down, which meant that the figure in black could pull out a mobile phone and make a call without fear of it getting soaked. They could only hope that there would be reception in the woods.

Dragging the bastard Loxley had been a pain, but now in the trees at the bottom of the Hollow, where the shallow valley walls levelled out and the flood water had ebbed away, the caller had found the perfect spot, both to dial and to do what had been hastily planned.

Again, the call was answered in a matter of seconds. 'Tell me you got it done this time,' said a voice.

'I'm about to,' replied the caller. 'The trees at the bottom of the Hollow—we are agreed?'

'Yes, yes. That sounds fine.'

They both knew that that way, Loxley would be found quickly, and things could get moving more quickly than if there was a search.

'So the edge of the woods would be best?' 'Yes.'

'I left her back up there.'

'Good. Do you have what you need?' 'Yes. Let's get this over with.'

'I'll leave you to it.'

The caller shut the call off and pocketed the phone, then took out a coil of thin blue rope. The end of it was already fashioned loosely into a noose, which was placed around Thor Loxley's neck.'You should have got on with it,' the figure said, and cackled darkly. 'You really should have got on with it. Shame that now, with the weight of it all, it had got so much that you felt you had to kill yourself.'

With a careful throw, the figure tossed the other bunched end of rope high into the tree over their heads, and watched as it fell over the crook of a couple of branches and back to the ground.

Loxley was still lying unconscious in the mud and dead leaves, the strike to the back of his head having got him good and proper.

The figure took a deep breath, feet placed wide apart, and pulled the rope through the branches, slowly at first, until there was resistance. Loxley's body weight.

With a mighty heave, Loxley was lifted slowly from the ground, and with a wracking snatch of coughed breath, his eyes flew open.

27

He was choking on something. In a dream. Something was stuck in his throat. He tried to dislodge it with a cough, but for some reason it only made his throat tighter.

He felt his head lift, as if some benevolent higher force was trying to sit him up to catch his breath, even if it only seemed to initially hurt more.

The hands that were helping him were rough and coarse, thin harsh fingers around his neck. He thought those hands shouldn't be there, that they should be under his arms or something. Because that grip around his neck was only making the choking worse.

Some clarity seemed to explode in his brain, an urgent and primal jolt of the instinct to survive and Thor's eyes flew open, as he was yanked slowly upright.

It was agony to breathe, and only a mere sliver of air was coming in with each frantic attempt; and the closer he got to his feet, the worse it became. The pain around his neck was severe, and suddenly became much worse as his toes lifted out of the shallow water at his feet. He looked down, which was a struggle, and could see that all around his feet were huge puddles, leaves, and dirt. The floor of the woods was gently flooded. He also saw that he was still just wearing his boxer shorts.

There was no air anymore, and his hands clawed at his throat. His lungs were a pulsing black hole in his chest, struggling to pump against a vacuum. His feet kicked involuntarily, causing him to spin slightly. As he turned, his vision caught the blurred zoetrope of the trees around him, and he thrashed blindly for air, purchase—anything that would stop this hell.

Thor wanted it to end. Nothing could be worse than this. Nothing. And then he saw the figure in black, straining against the rope,

pulling him slightly higher. He was being hanged.

Thor felt his body begin to spasm, but he was no longer able to control it. He reached out desperately to the figure, who had bent to tie the rope off around the tree. Thor wasn't going higher anymore, he just simply hung there, dying, and spinning ever so slowly.

He tried to squeeze his fingers between the noose and his neck, but it was too tight. Panic had now fully taken hold. He tried to reach high above his head to pull himself up the rope, but his arms were weak, burning branches attached to the burning stump that was his body.

His legs ran in mid-air, he clawed at his throat. And it seemed that, as horrible as it was to experience, it was just as awful to watch, as the figure in black did. It seemed to take two unsure steps backwards, before breaking into a sprint into the dark.

Leaving Thor hanging there, with no help, no salvation, no hope.

As he rotated slowly, he tried to think of anything to give him comfort as he passed away. His mind fixed on Roisin, and the happiness she gave him. He saw her in his mind's eye, smiling, her hair up, her glasses on. The warmth of her smile, and the heat of her lips he knew he would never touch again . . .

And then his foot touched something.

What was it? He thrashed his legs. There—again! He tried to focus. The tree he was hung from was closer somehow. He kicked his legs wildly—yes, he was getting closer to it, he saw its wet bark shimmering in the moonlight.

As he thrashed, the wet rope moved slickly along the branch it was looped over. He swung his legs and arms wildly, every ounce of his being concentrated on his one chance of survival.

He swung closer to the tree, and, seizing a chance, swung his legs frantically around it. The rough bark between his legs gave him just enough to grip with, and that in turn was just enough to allow him to

pull at the noose. He grabbed the thickly coiled knot and tugged it as hard as he could.

It gave, just enough for him to pull in a breath. He pulled again at the noose, one hand holding the rope up above the noose, the other on the knot itself. It got wider, slightly, inch by inch. It was up over his chin, then his mouth. It got stuck on his nose and top lip, shredding them raw, causing him to scream.

One last effort.

Over his nose, his eyes, scrubbing his forehead raw—and then suddenly it was off.

He fell, landing in the water with a splash. He lay there in a couple of inches of water, gasping, oxygen flooding his ravaged body. He had never felt so lucky.

This was supposed to be a suicide. He was supposed to be dead— again. Yet again he wasn't. He lay there, his very bone marrow icing over as adrenaline washed back into his blood.

An even colder fury brought it back full strength.

There was only one thing he could do. He was done with being a sitting duck, the one fish in the barrel.

It was time to go on the offensive.

28

Thor took a couple of moments to get his breath and his bearings back. Then he got up out of the water and began to run up the hill.

He grew more furious with every stride. Whoever had tried to kill him had tried to make it look like suicide. He'd been stripped of his clothes, his dignity (such as it was), and, had they succeeded, his family would have faced who knows how much guilt and trauma over what a tragic end he'd arrived at.

His rage was tempered by his fear about what may have happened to Roisin. There were two assailants, of that he'd been sure, and he'd only seen one. The other must have been with Roisin during that time, and if they wanted to kill Thor, what might they have done with her? She'd know that Thor hadn't killed himself. And that meant that as long as she was alive, the killers' plans couldn't succeed.

Thor upped his pace. The caravan loomed dark in the moonlight ahead, on the crest of the valley like a squat metal wolf baying at the moon high above. He hoped she was there. At the same time, he was terrified of what he might find. If the killers really wanted to make Thor look bad, they could leave Roisin dead in the caravan. That way, it would look as if Thor had killed her, then killed himself.

The thought was too awful to bear. He ran as fast as his bare feet would allow him.

Rounding the side of the caravan, the small yard lay empty—and Roisin's car was gone. He went to the front door and threw it open.

'Roisin?' No answer.

The living room was just how they had left it the night before: crumpled blankets, tea mugs, and spent candles. He turned to look down to the rear of the caravan, and the bedroom. The small corridor was obstructed by the door that he pushed through and lay flat on the floor, and he could see through to the bedroom beyond.

It was all as he remembered, and aside from the door, there was no sign of the struggle they had endured. But no Roisin. No sign of her. His fear hit another level.

What had they done to her? Where had they taken her?

In the bedroom, he found his clothes and dragged them on urgently, aware that he was awash with mud. He couldn't waste any time.

Then he noticed it, on the bed—the lamp Roisin had picked up. The wooden one he liked. It lay broken on the covers, a split running through the base and the Edison bulb hanging limp by its cable.

A sign of struggle. Roisin had been forced to defend herself.

He needed the police, and he needed them now. Roisin didn't have a landline out here, preferring to use her mobile phone. Where was it? He tossed the bedroom, then, having had no luck, searched through the rest of the caravan.

No phone.

When Roisin had been taken, had she taken it with her?

That was a thimbleful of hope. He could imagine Roisin being put in her car and driven away, but if she had her phone with her she could secretly call for help.

But that told him that even the most positive scenario meant she had most likely been kidnapped and could be killed.

Thor sat on the sofa, in the dark. He needed a second to get his head straight. He needed the police, but couldn't reach them.

The attacker. Thor was sure it was a man. The size was right. The voice in the field when he was attacked was a man's, unquestionably. The day after the first attack, Wendell said that the night before, he and his brother had been doing something that would upset the Loxleys.

The man in the woods could well have been Wendell or Ward. The build fit. And the fact that there were two of them would also fit the fact that there were two attackers.

It started to make sense.

He could only think that this was further proof of a plan between Clyne and the Crooks. They were the only people that would benefit from Thor's death.

That meant Roisin's own family would have to have been responsible for her disappearance, and God knows what else. He just couldn't see any alternative.

The Crooks were the snake. He was sure of it. And there was only one thing for a snake, if you wanted to stop it.

You had to cut off its head

29

Between the caravan and Crook's farm lay a flat quarter mile of potato fields bathed in almost purple moonlight. The farm sat like a distant compound, a Georgian farmhouse in the traditional mould, with whitewashed stone walls which seemed to glow in the lunar light. Three stories high, with a slate roof, it was a giant kids' building block left standing for generations.

Thor took the fields instead of the road, picking his way between rows of potato shoots, running as fast as he could. He imagined that Roisin's life hung in the balance, and he was running on pure adrenaline. He couldn't remember the last time he had eaten, or when he had last wanted to.

As he got closer to the main house, he tried to map out an entry. He needed to get in quickly and quietly. He had to find out where they were holding her, and then contact the police.

There were cars in the driveway. He didn't know who drove what, but given that there were five of them, each in different states of repair, he figured at least three or more people must be inside. Roisin's car, however, was nowhere to be seen.

The wind was still blowing heavily against the boughs of the trees, masking his footsteps. As he got closer to the windows, he saw how old they were—untempered single-frame glazing right around the house—perfect for a forced entry.

He needed to find a window into the kitchen, because that was where he would find a weapon—a knife, or something. Dogs would usually be a concern, but Roisin had said that they were not dog people these days, a notion Thor thought unlikely given the traditional farm culture that both the Crooks and Loxleys lived in. Every old farm had dogs.

He waited for his heart to stop hammering, and took a second to lean against the fencing at the rear end of the field. In a second, he was running to the ground-floor windows to the right of the front door.

He had taken all of two steps more when the security lights on the front of the house blinked on, almost blinding him. Shit, he thought, as he dipped low and made for the wall of the house. He was no cat burglar; if he survived the night, that wouldn't be a future career option.

He got to the stone wall and leaned back flush to it, the cool abrasiveness of the wall's surface a happy but brief respite to the tension across his shoulders. He waited for any sign that the Crooks were checking who was snooping around in the yard.

No movement, no sound. He counted slowly to ten. On five, the security light blinked off again.

Living at Loxley Farm, he was used to the security light coming on at all times of the night. Their yard had been a passing place for all manner of animals from the surrounding fields, and would trip the light regularly. It became routine, scarcely noticed, like the ticking of a living room clock.

He picked a stone from the abandoned potting beds beneath the window, one that would easily go through the glass. He could see little of the room beyond, as the room itself was obscured by the soft stitching of some ancient net curtains. Must be the kitchen, he thought.

At the last second, he thought about trying the front door instead, on the off chance it might be open—and in what could have been the first time Thor felt he had experienced any kind of good luck in a long time, the grand old door swung open quietly.

The sounds of the whirling breeze flooded through the opening gap into the house, so Thor snuck in as quickly as he could, pulling the door shut again behind him.

Silence, save for the soft whistle of wind coming through the gaps in more than one faulty old window seal. He took a couple of seconds to get his bearings—old stone floors just like Loxley farm, higher ceilings than expected with exposed beams throughout—and made his way into the kitchen.

He needed to find something that could subdue at least two people, possibly more. A single knife couldn't do that, so he filled the kettle and set it to boil. There had been a spate of burglaries in the area a couple of years ago, where the intruders entered empty handed and used hot kettles and the threat of boiling water sprayed about to get what they wanted. Every house had one, the weapon was already there, and nothing—no man, woman, or child likes boiling water. It made Thor's skin itch at the thought of having to use it, but it would have to do.

While the kettle boiled, Thor looked for something to shield his face—even though he was supposed to be dead, he might as well get the advantages of being dead for a while.

There was a tea towel on the oven handle, which he wrapped around his head. Too tight and small. On the back of the kitchen door was some coats, hats and a couple of scarfs. He took one, looped it twice round the bottom half of his face, and pulled a woolen hat on so that all that was visible was nose and eyes. It would do.

The kettle boiled and he took it up the stairs. Half of him was fascinated at being in the Crooks' house, with the ghosts of past generations haunting the same rooms he, a Loxley, was now in. The other half was struggling to beat back the sharks of panic that were circling in his guts.

Get Roisin back became a silent mantra. The stairs were wide, stone and imposing, doubling back on themselves at a wide landing. The house was deeply quiet, and the heavy stone didn't betray his footsteps.

Thor needed to make sure he knew who was in the house, so he checked every room on the second floor, before moving up to the third. He heard heavy snoring from the door at the end, so he resolved to leave that for last. There were four other doors in the hallway, which he checked one after the other.

The first was a bathroom with bare wood floors and a claw-foot tub standing regally on a raised platform beneath the window.

Door two led to a bedroom that looked as though it belonged to a teenager from the 1980s. There were posters of Duran Duran, and Sam Fox. One of Kelly Kapowski, from Saved By The Bell. There was an old flatpack wooden shelving set, which housed an ancient PC. On another shelf was a crusted fish tank, which looked to contain no life whatsoever, but was surely one of the contributors to the smell: a nearly overwhelming sweetness of rot.

Thor would have thought it was a room abandoned in time, but the bed was clearly recently used, half of it strewn with jackets, jeans, work boots, socks. This was either Ward's or Wendell's room. If he'd had to guess, he'd have attached this bizarre setup to the unhinged Ward. And worse still—he wasn't here.

He tried the next door, which was a contrast. It was clean, for a start. Fitted wardrobes lined the wall over the bed, with a huge flat- screen TV mounted opposite it. There were no posters, and this was not the room of any teenage boy, past or present. Books lined the shelves—titles on agriculture, poetry, and travel. Topics, at a glance, like optimum conditions for a successful radish harvest, seafood dining guides in South East Asia, the complete illustrated works of William Wordsworth. Wendell.

It was a bewildering if fascinating insight into the two brothers, who evidently shared genetic composition and general mindset, but precious little else.

And again, the room was empty. Thor was now convinced. In their absence, he had found his adversaries.

The penultimate door Thor opened carefully, aware that the likelihood of meeting inhabitants was getting higher with every room. But his caution didn't remotely prepare him for what he saw.

It belonged to another teenager, a girl this time. The bed was made, but looked starchy and faded in its rest. The teddies around the pillows were perfectly arranged, yet cobwebbed and dusty. The old wardrobes opposite the bed had finger tracks through the dust around the handles, suggesting they had been opened recently. Thor couldn't help but look, and found clothes. Some of them were sportswear and tracksuits, with pink fringing and stripes, while some were jet black, in gothic cuts.

There was a fireplace, long since filled in, but the mantel above it carried a couple of photographs. A girl, seventeen or so. Her dyed black hair streaked back from her head and tinged with a fiery red at the tips. She wore a long-sleeved black jumper and a broad but less than happy smile.

Thor took a step back, looking at the mantelpiece as a whole. The old room, untouched, the placement of the photo frames...

The is no ordinary room, thought Thor. This is a shrine.

The identity of the girl was a mystery. Logic dictated it had to be Roisin's room, but the girl in the photographs, despite similarities, wasn't her. He thought immediately that it must a cousin, or relative. But that wouldn't tally with the room as it presently stood. The eyes and cheeks were familiar, it looked like they carried history in them.

The girl was a Crook. She looked like Ward, Wendell, and Roisin, especially Roisin, in small, almost indefinable, but definite ways.

A sibling that they had lost? Why did he not know about this? Had he somehow missed this?

Roisin had an older sister?

What this meant, if true, was unclear, but if nothing else it added a distinctly complicated layer to the complexion of the Crooks.

He left the room as he had found it, taking with him only the haunting mental picture of the girl in the pictures.

The snoring was still thundering from the room at the end of the hall. He opened the door with care.

It was a huge bedroom, very tidy, and rich: cream carpets, more high beams, a standing mirror by an ornate wooden dresser, with simple dark wood wardrobes on either side of a grand, high brass-framed bed.

Thor crept closer. On the left side of the bed lay an old man with his head back and his mouth so wide Thor thought he could throw an 8-ball straight down the man's throat without touching his teeth.

He had never seen Mason Crook this close before, having only

seen him at a distance just a few times in his youth, and now his former apprehensions of the man bloomed in his chest. The stories he had heard were those of a formidable taskmaster, monstrous worker, and epic drinker, none of which tallied with the snoring old geezer in the bed. And just to dent the image that bit further, there was an oxygen tank behind the bed, a face mask dangling from the pressure valve.

'What do you want?' a frail female voice said. 'Take what you want and get out.'

The voice didn't wake Mason, and Thor, remembering why he was there, raised the kettle high over the bed.

'Answer my questions, and I won't pour this all over you both,' he said, trying to add a lower octave to his voice, to make himself seem imposing.

'Is that boiling water?' asked Tilly Crook, the matriarch of the Crook family. In her late seventies, she lay beneath the white quilt in an equally white nightgown, her silver hair up on rollers on the pillow. Her face was drawn tight at the chin by the gaunting of time. There was a tone of sorrow and sadness in her voice, the unyielding stoicism of a farm woman of her generation.

'Yep, and I'll start chucking it about if you don't tell me what I need to know.' He was glad for the scarf covering his face, because at the very least it masked the tremor on his cheeks.

Get Roisin back. Get Roisin back.

'OK,' said Tilly, placatingly. Mason still shuddered the walls with his snoring.

'Where is Roisin?'

Tilly's eyes opened wide. 'Roisin? Why, what's happened?' 'You tell me. Now.'

'I don't know. I mean it. I assume she's in her caravan, have you checked there?'

'Ward and Wendell have taken her. Where have they taken her to?

You know what I'm taking about, so don't make me explain it again.' 'I'm afraid I really don't.'

Thor flicked water from the kettle at the dresser, steam drifting out, the boiling liquid hissing as it hit the wood.

'The land deal with Clyne. You're accepting it, aren't you?'

Tilly didn't hesitate. 'Wouldn't anybody? We are too old for this farm. The offer gives our family security for the rest of our lives.'

'But you need Thornton Loxley dead, don't you? Is that why you've been trying to kill him?'

'I don't know who's been trying kill who, but none of that has been coming from us. None of it. And as for Roisin, she's a big enough girl to look after herself, don't you think?'

'Give me Roisin. Last chance.' Thor raised the kettle again, and Tilly watched, again with an expression of resignation. Thor was faced with the moment of truth: whether to douse the old woman in boiling water, and become everything he hated.

The decision was made for him. Beyond the curtained windows, the security light on the front drive came on, heralded by a spray of gravel and the gargle of an old motor.

Someone was home.

Suddenly a huge blast threw Thor backwards in shock. It was as if a mortar or a bomb had gone off in the bedroom. Feathers were raining from the ceiling. Mason scrambled to his feet in shock and confusion, and Tilly sat up from under the now-shredded quilt—and pulled a shotgun out of the bedclothes.

She had had it trained on him the whole time, beneath the covers, between her and Mason.

'Thor's in here,' she shouted. 'Up here, boys, Mummy's bedroom!'

Thor, deafened by the blast, had barely registered her words when to his horror the barrel came up and she fired again.

Thor flung himself aside in time, stumbled, and fell to his knees. He scrambled for the door. He heard Tilly clicking two more shells into the shotgun's chambers.

Thor was down the hall in a couple of seconds, but his escape was cut off: two men were running up the stairs towards him. He threw the kettle down at the figures, which sprayed hopeless drops as it fell, but they were wrapped in coats and winter clothes. They navigated the stairs with ease, as if they had done it a thousand times before.

Wendell and Ward.

Thor took the stairs leading up, and bounded two at a time. The voices behind were animatedly out instructions.

'The Remington and the Philadelphia Fox—get them now, I've got your mother's Birmingham Box.'

It was Mason Crook, coordinating the action. 'He can't go nowhere from here. Only way down is the stairs. It'll be no more complicated than ratting.'

The brothers retreated down the stairs as Thor got to the top. He noticed that Mason had used the guns' names. Like his eldest brother, Wilkes VIII, the Crooks were fans of vintage shotguns.

So there were three guns out for him, versus his none.

The top of the stairs terminated in a small landing with just two doors to pick from, and Thor knew from experience that they must be old grain stores. In more primitive farming times, grain was kept up high, out of reach of the vermin at ground level. Thor took the left door and hoped there would be something in there that at least he could hide behind.

Opening it, he encountered a cave. A stage was set up, ready for a metal band to drop in and shake the building to its ancient foundations. There were huge Marshall amps looming up at the far end of the room, either side of a full drum kit, a couple of fearsome looking guitars, and a keyboard and a couple of microphones. The situation had taken another weird tilt, but Thor had no time to consider it. He ran for the amps.

As he came deeper into the room he saw that to the right of the door was a bar, set up and ready to host, optics lining the back wall and a couple of ale pumps facing forward. Couches separated the two ends of the room. Apparently the Crook brothers, despite being in their forties and living at home with their parents, still harboured dreams of being rock stars, and lived accordingly—in their grain loft.

Thor hid behind the stack of amps on the right. There was a window behind him where he crouched, but all it led to was three stories of cold air. He was trapped.

He settled as quietly as he could behind the amp, looking for something, anything, that could be used as a weapon. The only thing he could see was one of the guitars, a 'flying V' model with a two- pronged lower body. He grabbed it by the neck and pulled it behind the amp with him.

The door creaked open. Thor instinctively held his breath.

'This one,' he heard someone whisper. Thor guessed it was Mason, given the authoritative tone.

'You're sure it's Loxley?' the other asked quietly. 'That's who your mother said it was,' replied Mason. 'Shit. How?'

This was it. He was cornered, and they'd have no qualms about killing him now.

'… I don't know,' Mason continued, 'but he's trespassing. And the law's in our hands now. Extra bowl of porridge for whoever takes him out.'

Thor watched in the reflection of the window as the door opened fully, and three long shotgun barrels poked in, catching shards of moonlight as they swung. He struggled to keep his breathing in check. He was truly fucked. Gunned down in the Crooks' loft. With sick humour he marveled at what a great chapter this would be in the fabled history of the two families and their problems—he just wished he wasn't the main character.

The awful possibility was dawning on him that Roisin was now dead, and he had to push the dreaded thought aside. If Roisin had been killed by her two brothers, there was precious little else for Thor to live for—abut still the very thought made hum angry. He watched as the guns in the reflection came steadily into the room.

A kernel of pride popped in his chest. He wasn't going down here—not to this lot. He was a Loxley, and if there was any true Loxley left in him, he'd do anything to avoid being beaten by the Crooks. Anything at all.

He leaned against the amp, trying to think, and pulled the scarf from his head. The reflection still painted a bleak picture.

The reflection: the glass. The weak, thin single-glazed pane, just like everywhere else in the house.

The amp behind him was solid against his spine, and he looked down. The thick power cable was lying by his left heel, wound tight, and snaked to a socket in the wall. He crouched, put both hands on the socket, and took a deep breath.

Stupid, he thought, and in one motion he ripped the plug out of the wall, wrapped the cable twice round his wrist, and threw himself at the window.

Three things happened almost at once: Thor impacted the window, which shattered; there was a deafening blast; and glass and plaster bits and wood splinters filled the air.

Thor quickly twisted the cable more tightly around his wrist as he fell, barely aware of the glass in his hair, feeling only the cold air whistling around his body as he fell straight down. In no time at all, his right arm suddenly snapped back up to the sky, as the cable went tight on the weight of the amp. The cable juddered out of Thor's grip, and then there was quick agony as the cable was yanked tight against his bare skin. He screamed, something seemed to pop in his arm, and he fell the last ten feet into a setup of patio furniture.

Pieces of white plastic furniture seemed to explode in every direction. The flying V guitar landed with a clatter of cracking wood. A security light flashed on, blinding him, but he knew he had no time—none. Not now he had resolved to live through it. He rolled in agony, putting weight on his right hand but wishing he hadn't.

He scrambled to his feet and ran as buckshot rained down from above, each blast lighting up the night for a moment. He looked for the nearest patch of darkness, and ran to it, hobbling and gasping. The patch of trees he found were thick enough to mask him, but he knew he couldn't stop.

If his bearings were right, pressing though the trees would take him in the general direction of Crook's Hollow, and a slight course change to his left would bring him out, three miles later, at Loxley Farm. The only sanctuary he could imagine was at his father's side, so busted, broken, and God knows what else, he got to marching.

30

High above Thor, the last shot rang out. Wendell reached in his jacket for more shells, but his father stopped him with a finger on his forearm.

'No, let him go,' he said.

Ward was incredulous. 'We can't let him go, not now we've tried to kill him.'

'He was trespassing, it was his own fault. He's not going to the police, he broke in here first. The police are stupid, but they know which side their bread is buttered on around here.'

'Do you think he'll tell anyone?' asked Wendell.

'If he does, it'll be big problems. It's a good job we are selling up and getting out. But I don't think it will.'

'If it even was Thor Loxley,' Wendell said.

'If it even was Thor Loxley,' repeated his father. 'But if it really was, I wish we'd got him. One last gift for that bastard Wilkes before we go.' They watched the figure limp through the trees, Ward raging because he felt sure he could still take the intruder out from where they stood. Loxley was becoming less of a fly in the ointment and

more like a fucking albatross.

31

As dawn began to break, while the sun edged higher to a bank of thick black cloud that was just waiting to swallow it up and send the day into torrents once again, there was a brief, beautiful window of clear sunlight.

Perfect time to discover a body.

The searcher picked Wellington boots this time, fully aware of how difficult the terrain had been the night before, but also acknowledging that the bulk of standing water would have drained off by now. The searcher's prints were important, and it was vital that this went according to plan.

This was the last chance, and every box had to be ticked, crossed, checked, signed—whatever. It had to be perfect.

As soon as the body was seen, some 'panicky' footsteps were called for. Then some long strides back out of the wood, to simulate a nice sprint to call in the authorities.

Just through the first trees, that's what the instructions were. Not far in.

The searcher took a moment to prepare, because the sight wouldn't be a pleasant one. Hangings were always supposed to be grim: the unnatural way the body swings in space, upright but apart. And it could only be especially worse if you'd known the person.

It must be close by. But where?

The searcher suddenly worried that the body had fallen down and been dragged away by scavengers. That would be another needless spanner in the works, as if there hadn't been enough going wrong already.

It must be here. But where? Where—

And then the searcher did find something, but it wasn't what was expected.

Softly swinging, framed almost artistically by the frittering boughs above, was a noose. An empty one.

There was no need to pretend to run back up the hill in a panic, because that is exactly what the owner of the Wellies did.

32

The rain had just begun to fall again, in lazy, fat drops, when Thor made it into the yard at Loxley Farm. He was exhausted but alive. Very much alive. He knocked on the front door, hoping someone was up— he was dead tired.

The door was answered by Hollis, who on seeing Thor, immediately rolled his eyes. 'Oh shite… Dad!' he called.

'Don't look so thrilled,' Thor muttered as he pushed past him.

The kitchen had been patched up, and there was a new stone in place over the well, held down by fresh cement. They had done a great job. You'd never know there'd been a problem; the kitchen, save for the new stone, was just as it had been before. Even the traditions were back in force, as the family was eating breakfast around the table, together as always, save for Rue, Barry, and their kids, who were in their bungalow, and Wilkes Jr., Theresa and their kids, who were at their home in the village.

A collective gasp arose at the sight of Thor and his obvious injuries, with Bunny jumping up as quickly as her frame would allow. Wilkes Sr. stood immediately, genuine concern on his face.

'Oh, for God's sake, Thornton,' Bunny snapped with a sliver of concern embedded in her disappointment. 'What the bloody hell have you been doing now?'

Thor sat down gently, the pain in his ribs spiraling across his chest. 'Pass me the phone... Hollis—the phone.'

Hollis, who had almost sat back down to his breakfast, huffed like a teenager told he was going to grandma's for the day. From the counter, he tossed Thor the phone. Thor fumbled with his left hand and just about caught it.

'Watch it, you fucking idiot,' he said.

'Thornton,' admonished his mother, but Thor was already dialing the number on the filthy business card he had pulled from his pocket.

'Not now,' Thor said.

Wilkes Sr. came to his son's side, and looked at his wounds. Thor's face was a mess of small nicks and cuts, the odd bit of fresh purple mixing nastily with the yellow of the old bruises from a couple of nights back. Much skin was missing from the tip of his nose. There was a much darker purple on Thor's right wrist, snaking up onto his hand. His neck most concerned Wilkes: it was shredded in more than one place, and looked like the job had been done with a cheese grater.

'Yes, hello, Okpara?' Thor said. 'Yes, it's Thor Loxley. Remember, someone was trying to kill me? I know who it is, I've just got away from there now. It was Ward and Wendell Crook of Crook's Farm, and they were helped by their parents Tilly and Mason Crook.'

Every person at the table looked at Thor, dumbfounded. Thor continued.

'They tried to hang me in the woods down in Crook's Hollow, then when that didn't work, they shot at me with shotguns… Yes, I think I know why now. Land. It's about land and who has it.'

Mercy Loxley stood up, still holding a fork, while chewing fiercely on a piece of toast. Her gaze was fire.

'I believe they've got Roisin hidden away. She's their daughter... Well, she's gone missing is all I know... No, I know she has gone missing. You have to find her.'

The family looked at one another in increasing confusion. Wilkes Sr. took a step back to the countertop behind him, listening intently.

'Yes, she was at her caravan above Crook's Hollow. I was staying with her when we were attacked. They tried to make it look like a suicide in the woods, but I escaped and when I got back to the caravan they had taken Roisin—they must have, otherwise she would not have left me. I tried to get her back, but that's when they started shooting. And I need an ambulance because I think my wrist is broken... No, I'm not going to hospital, so you'll have to send it up to Loxley Farm. Yes, I'll wait here. OK, I'll see you then.'

When Thor hung up, the room was thick with atmosphere. A moment hung between them while all that could be heard were Thor's ragged breaths.

'Was that all true?' asked Crewe, standing at the head of the table with his fists balled at his sides.

'Every word,' said Thor. 'They tried to kill me on Saturday night, too, and it was them at church on Sunday. They want me dead because they believe my portion of land is the only thing stopping them getting paid.'

Silence, full and deadly.

Thor caught his mother's eye. She was regarding him with what looked like deep sadness: there was so much they could all have done differently over the years—different decisions could have avoided this turn of events.

'We need to get to them,' said Mercy with grit.

'The police are bringing them in,' said Thor. 'That was the DCI, he's going for them personally, then he's coming here.'

Hollis sat down again, and dipped a finger of toast into a boiled egg. 'Bloody hell, Thor,' he muttered with a small grin. 'You know just how to stir it.'

The room seemed to cool, but Wilkes Sr. suddenly appeared at Thor's side. He stood looking fixedly at the floor, avoiding Thor's eyes.

'Roisin, the young Crook girl,' he said. 'What were you doing there?'

Thor couldn't believe it. He'd nearly been killed and all his father was interested in was the same old Loxley–Crook rubbish, the same rubbish that had plagued the families for generations.

'What do you think Dad? Jesus, want me to spell it out?'

Wilkes Sr was silent, intent: he seemed to be picking his words as carefully as he could. 'You can't,' he finally said.

'Bloody hell, give over. Same old rubbish.' 'You can't, Thor.'

'Yeah, well, you might be in luck if she's dead. That make you any happier?'

Thor got up and went to the sink and washed his face. 'You want a cup of tea?' Hollis asked.

'That's the most sensible thing you've ever said to me,' said Thor, nodding

33

Fifteen minutes later, an ambulance arrived. No sirens, to Thor's gratitude. The heavens had opened once more, soaking the drive into a swamp again, and as the ambulance pulled in, mud sprayed up onto its flanks.

The paramedics tended to Thor in the kitchen, which had become a kind of Loxley war room. The siblings sat around the table, swapping plans which sounded like grim fantasies of what they would do if they got their hands on the Crooks again. Wilkes Jr. came over after Hollis gave him the heads-up. It was as if the attempts on Thor's life were just the thing they had been waiting for to go after the Crooks.

In contrast, Wilkes Sr. simply stared out of the window, looking morose, as if he had always known it might come to this and wished it hadn't.

Thor sat by the door, on a chair his mother had dragged over, and let the medics do their job. Three broken ribs, they said. One broken wrist with a damaged tendon in his forearm, which they thought had been torn. A badly bruised hip, and kidney bruising. A neck strain, not to mention a badly cut neck that might well be infected. In short, a hospital trip was badly needed.

Thor refused, remembering how easily Clyne appeared at his bedside. 'I was promised protection last time, and that didn't happen. You'll have to patch me up here.'

The two medics looked at each other, and resignedly got to work. They started with morphine injections, and a drip. The kitchen began to now look part war room, part emergency triage.

Rue appeared at the front door, her hood pulled up against the rain. 'What's happening? I saw the ambulance and—oh my God, Thor...' Her features crumpled on seeing Thor and she came to his side. He smiled sleepily, the morphine doing its job.

'Hello sis,' he said.

'Thor, what happened this time?' she said, casting her eyes about him, taking in the extent of his injuries, tears brimming more as she counted each one.

'The Crooks. But it's OK, they are going after them. The police, I mean.' He waved his hand in the general direction of Crook's Farm.

'The Crooks did this?' Rue said, looking at their siblings around the table, knowing full well the chain of events that this could start. She was met with stern faces, and a grim nod from Mercy.

'They've got Roisin,' said Thor. 'What do you mean?'

'They tried to kill me, make it look like a suicide, and they took Roisin.'

'Oh my God, I can't believe any of this.'

'Then you'll have to catch up. They'll find her though. They have to. I need her.'

Thor looked as if he might fall asleep, so Rue stood and took her little brother's head against her hip.

'It's alright, they'll find her. Rest now, it'll be OK. Rue's here.' She patted his head like she used to when they were children.

Thor smiled dreamily. He hadn't heard that since he was a child, and it made him feel better than any morphine in the world.

34

The day laboured along in one of those maternity ward pauses, where there is so much ready to happen, but you can't start yet. When he'd settled, and Rue had gone home to her kids, Thor spent a lot of it in the family room on the couch, in and out of sleep, using a dog he'd never met before as a duvet. The dog, Lily, was only too happy to oblige, and watched the rain plink the window. Wilkes Sr. had made a fire for Thor and every now and then he checked on both the hearth and his son.

Bunny sat opposite in an armchair, knitting and tutting to herself. She managed to knit two full scarves and a woolly hat before Hollis came in to announce that DCI Okpara had arrived.

'Bring him into the family room,' said Wilkes Sr. 'And offer him a hot drink.'

Thor tried to sit up, but it was almost too much of an effort. He was drowned by exhaustion and the blissful opiates, and he slumped. He was lucid, but subdued. Okpara came in, along with a constable, and Bunny showed them to the other armchair. Wilkes Sr. loitered by the door, his nervous energy holding him ramrod straight.

'Thor, how are you feeling?' Okpara asked. He was dressed in a grey suit, shirt and tie, no shoes just socks. As he put his raincoat down, Thor caught sight of a brightly coloured belt made of small beads around his waist. It looked traditional, and stood at odds with the rest of his otherwise formal attire.

'I'm OK,' said Thor. 'I would say I've been worse, but that would be a flat-out lie. Tell me you found her.'

'Thor, there are various formalities to address now, but the first is we need a full and proper statement.' His calming manner threatened to join the dregs of the opiates in forcing Thor into compliance, but he dragged himself back.

'Why are you avoiding the question? Have you found her?'

'No, Thor, we haven't. That is not to say she isn't missing, but she wasn't at home when we called.'

'I know she's not home, I told you that. Her brothers took her.' 'Thor, they couldn't have. That's what I'm trying to tell you. The Crook family have taken nobody.' He spread his hands in a gesture of open fairness.

'What do you mean? Didn't you listen to what I told you before? They need me dead for the land deal with COMUDEV to go through, they've been trying to kill me and make it look like an accident for days now. Didn't you hear any of that?'

'Thor, they came in voluntarily for questioning this morning. They gave a full account of their movements over the last few days, last night included. I've personally checked their alibis—they are all good. They didn't attack you last night. What they did admit to was defending themselves from a man who entered their property threatening them with a kettle of boiling water. What do you know about that?'

Wilkes Sr. couldn't pull his eyes from the rug in front of the hearth, while Bunny click-clacked through her knitting. However, Thor knew from the expression on her face that she was living every word of the conversation.

265

'You've got a missing girl and you want to talk about this? You're joking, aren't you? Tell me you're joking.'

'I'm afraid I'm not. We have spent the afternoon at the Crooks' property assessing the validity of their claims, and every word of it tallies up. I know you think they are responsible for your current problems, but after interviewing them extensively, I am forced to conclude that they are not.'

'How do you fathom that? How?'

'Like I said Thor, their alibis are sound. Right through every occasion you say there was an attempt on your life.'

'So where is Roisin? Where the hell is she? If they didn't take her, who did?'

Thor was becoming doubly furious now, feeling that Okpara had wasted a whole day instead of looking for her. She could be long dead by now.

'Thor, it is getting to the point where I think the authorities have every right to ask you that same question. Do you know where Roisin Crook is?'

'No, you idiot, no.' Thor began to pull himself to his feet, but his balance was far from perfect. 'If you're not doing anything to find her, then I'm wasting no more time here.'

'Sit down, Mr. Loxley,' said Okpara, rising himself. 'You will wait until we've finished and you will kindly answer the question.'

Thor slowly sat down, and Okpara continued.

'I don't doubt that there have been some very difficult moments for you in the past few days, Thor, and we will continue to look into them—I will continue to look into them personally. But the avenue you suggested isn't correct. Furthermore, it has led to another crime that I'm afraid I have to continue investigating, namely the unlawful entry of Crook's Farm last night, and the threats and assaults that followed.'

Thor was speechless, but only for a second.

'Roisin could be lying in the fucking gutter somewhere, or chained to a pipe in some basement, or lying long dead in a field getting her eyes pecked out by magpies, and this is what you want to talk about.'

Okpara spoke quietly and with authority. 'Mr. Loxley, you will settle down and assist in my enquiries. Your assertion that Roisin Crook is missing has been duly noted, and already been followed up. We have visited her place of residence, and are satisfied that nothing untoward appears to have happened to her.'

'The door, what about the door? And the broken lamp?' 'We saw no such things.'

'What the fuck are you talking about? They were there! I saw them!'

'To be classed as missing, usually the next of kin alerts the police that someone is in fact missing. The Crooks have done no such thing. They are not concerned in any way about Roisin's whereabouts. Apparently unannounced absences are a regular thing with her. Her mother referred to her as free-spirited, which I thought was an exceptionally understanding way for a mother to view things. They are convinced she will turn up in due course.'

'Of course they'd bloody say that. That's what serial killers say when they've got a body hidden somewhere.'

'Mr Loxley, did you enter the Crooks' property last night?' 'You know I did.'

'Did you throw boiling water around by way of intimidation?'

Thor took a second, but he knew somehow, despite everything that had happened, that he was cornered. 'I did, but I was trying to find Roisin.'

'Then I'm very sorry, Thor, but you leave me very little choice. Thor Loxley, I'm arresting you for unlawful entry and attempted assault. You do not have to say anything. But, it may harm your defence if you do not mention when questioned something which you later rely on in court. Anything you do say may be given in evidence.'

'You're kidding. You are fucking kidding.'

Okpara nodded to the constable. 'Are we about to have a problem, Thor? You can come with me quietly and avoid any dramas.'

'You know someone has been trying to kill me, why can't you see that? Why aren't you helping me?'

'I do see that, Thor. There is no doubt in my mind that someone has committed criminal acts against you. One can tell that just from looking at you. But I'm equally concerned with protecting you and others from yourself. Let's go.'

Wilkes Sr. finally spoke up. 'Should I arrange a visit from the family solicitor?'

'That's up to Thor, Mr Loxley,' replied Okpara. 'Between the four of us I'd suggest that would be a good idea.'

'I don't need one.'

The constable took Thor's arm and they started walking to the door of the family room. His mother stopped them. She placed the woollen hat she had just knitted on his head.

'It's cold out,' she said. 'Call us when you can.' She looked more confused than anything, as if the moment was so beyond her comprehension all she could do was cling to whatever familiarity felt right, which in this case was her knitting.

'Dad, please,' Thor said, as the officer led him through the kitchen and out to the yard, while his siblings turned and watched. 'I don't care about me, but Roisin is in trouble. You have to find her. Dad, please. You have to help Roisin.'

Wilkes Sr. looked at him with resignation. The sad story of Thor, his youngest son, was taking an unexpected and even sadder turn than he had ever imagined.

35

Thor was driven to the station by a particularly lippy local bobby, who seemed thrilled to be involved in the big local case. Thor, however, was so despondent and confused he could only watch the rain, and try to work out how on earth it had got to this. Deep down he knew that it was his hot-headedness, anger, and poor judgement which had put him here. And it seemed more likely than ever that he had put Roisin in even greater danger.

'Raining cats and dogs is an understatement,' said the constable. 'More like raining tigers and wolves.'

Thor wondered how many times the PC had cracked that appalling gag over the past couple of days. All he could say was: 'The village is fucked, mate. In more ways than one.'

'That's one way of looking at it. DCI Okpara is waiting for you at the station in Windle Heath, you can tell him all about it.'

Thor looked through to the front seats of the police car. The PC was in his late twenties, short back'n'sided and positively electrified with what he was doing. He had introduced himself as PC Chesters.

'Interesting place, Crook's Hollow,' Chesters continued, eyeing Thor in the rearview mirror. 'Must have been mad growing up in it, 'specially in your position. I'm from Windle Heath myself.'

'They sound pretty similar on the face of it,' Thor said laconically. 'Hmm, not sure about that.' Chesters whipped through the

available radio stations, looking for a signal. 'Weather's even buggered the radio.'

Thor was in a cynical mood. 'Even the coke from Windle Heath's

ended up down here. Place is turning into a cesspool.'

'Wouldn't be so sure. Word on the street is that them Crook twins were the first to start peddling anything into the Heath, never mind the Hollow. The higher-ups have had an eye on them for years, but never anything to go on. Farmers—hard to pin down the lot of you. Having said that, even I was surprised with last night, what them brothers were up to.'

Thor was suddenly attentive. 'Sorry?'

'Yeah, them Crook brothers. Like the DCI told you, their alibi.'

Thor wanted Chesters to keep spilling, but didn't want to suggest that he was revealing things Okpara hadn't mentioned. 'Yeah, bloody hell. Who'd have thought,' he said, without having a clue.

'It's always the quiet ones, and it's always right under your nose.

That's probably the most important thing I've learned doing the job.' 'I can imagine,' said Thor. 'Where was it again?'

'Just round the corner from Sainsbury's—little two-up two-downer at bottom of Belsey Avenue. Why, are you thinking of popping down there after your chat with Okpara?' Chesters smiled laddishly.

'I wish,' said Thor.

'I wouldn't worry. Grannies, apparently that's all they had. Well, all that were on last night. Don't know whether they up their game at the weekend. Hey, could be your thing for all I know.'

Thor couldn't put his finger on it but a particular dirty picture was appearing in his mind.

'I promise you though, if you admit to that as your alibi, then God's honest truth, you definitely didn't do that crime. No chance.'

Another unexpected layer was peeling away from the brothers, one of lurid nighttime visits and secret lives begrudgingly dragged into the light.

'What do places like that get called these days?'

'Oh, all sorts. Nunnery's one. Cathouse's another. Bordello's a bit old now, I always thought it sounded quite continental and cosmopolitan, that. I'm a big fan of "meat locker" myself.'

A brothel.

'Did the ladies there confirm the alibi?'

'Oh, did they ever. The brothers said that's where they were, and when the hookers were interviewed, three of them confirmed it, and said they were with them. At the same time. As in the three whores, the two brothers. All at it. Together. In the same room. Kinky buggers.'

'Jesus.'

'Jesus wept, I'd say. I've been thinking why ever since I heard, and I think it's because they look the same. It's like watching yourself getting off, while getting off yourself. Kinky buggers. Amazing really.'

The constable was clearly enjoying his thought process.

Thor breathed out. That could throw a huge problem into his conclusions, unless the strippers were paid to provide the alibi. But like Chesters said, why would you admit to that stuff? Something was wrong. Everything was wrong.

'I wonder what Okpara makes of it?'

'Okpara? Man's a beast.' Chesters laughed but there was a very serious edge to it.

Thor continued treading gently. 'Yeah, of course, but, you know, what does he think of it? The alibi?'

'I dunno. Quiet man, but I don't second-guess him. One solid, solid bastard.'

That wasn't the picture that Thor had formed of the detective. Yes, he commanded respect, but that didn't quite fit.

'How'd you mean?' Thor asked.

'Well, look at him for a start,' Chesters said, betraying the deep- rooted little-Englishness that Thor was familiar with. In quiet places like this, where the wheels turn very slowly, he could imagine the more bigoted corners of Crook's Hollow and Windle Heath had very specific ideas about a black man holding such an important role in the region. 'Plus, he's a Masai, isn't he?'

'Is he?'

'Yeah, story goes he came over here right after he'd done his initiations into manhood, whatever they call that. Came over here looking for money for his family and ended up a cabbie.'

It was a hell of a story, and Thor couldn't help respect it. The adversity he must have faced to get to where he was… But that didn't stop him thinking that Okpara was wrong not to pursue Roisin's disappearance.

'What about Roisin?' he asked. 'Has she been found yet?'

'Oh yeah… Well, she's not turned up, but her parents aren't worried. They say this is standard behaviour for her. I wouldn't worry yourself either.

By all accounts, she'll be home before dinner. Their words, not mine.'

Thor felt helpless, and his anger swelled again.

'Why is nobody taking my story seriously? Do you think all this just happened to me?' Thor gestured at his face.

'You fell out of a third-story window didn't you, mate? I'd say it matches up. If anything you should be a hell of a lot worse.'

'We were attacked, the pair of us. They tried to kill me and make it look like a suicide, and all you lot want to do is swap the lurid stories and the choicer details.'

Chesters said nothing.

'I know. Do you want a real bit of juice, a real piece of the action? You want to see the noose? You want me to show you where it happened? I bet Okpara saw it, but I bet you didn't, did you? Not allowed at the big boys' table yet, are you?'

Chesters bristled visibly, the flags of his pride dancing to attention in the stiff breeze of Thor's words.

'You want the story for once, not the third-hand scraps? You like a bit of gossip, don't you? Well, you can dine out on this one for months. Come on, take the next right. Don't you want it?'

Chesters' cheeks burnt crimson, and thirteen minutes later they were marching through the young trees at the base of the Hollow, now both in high-visibility police all-weather jackets since Chesters had a spare in the boot of his patrol car.

They marched through the never-ending rain, now flush in their faces, as if it was spitting up windswept from a vast lake in front of them. As Thor led the way, they could both see that the terrain was more river than lake. The flood water was back, but now heavier, roiling with a dark, swirling intent. It was six inches deep, and their feet were soaked.

Thor used the tree line, and its growing scarcity, to navigate to the spot he was nearly killed, and as he got closer, his pace slowed.

'Where is it then?' asked Chesters, looking thoroughly nonplussed at the journey and the reality they had found, or rather not found: the noose was gone. Chesters laughed with bleak satisfaction, while Thor knew the truth.

Someone had cleaned the scene up.

They'd come back and erased it from ever happening, ably helped by nature. If this were summer, or any normal day, there'd be prints galore, crisp and clear.

'It has to be here,' muttered Thor. He was looking for any kind of mark in the trees, high up, where a rope would have abraded the wet bark and left a sign. But last night he was concussed, and literally being hung—the last thing he gave a shit about at that point was his precise location.

As he looked up, his hopes of showing Chester that he was telling the truth washing away with the speeding flood, a white-hot branch of lightning fractured the sky.

'We're going,' said Chesters, just as the thunder hit. Six seconds. Thor had counted six seconds between the lightning strike and the rumble of thunder. It was a habit forged in childhood, the rough principle being that a second equaled a mile. Therefore, if it was accurate, the storm was six miles away.

'It happened,' Thor shouted to Chesters, but his words were lost in the drum of the storm. Thor started begrudgingly to follow Chesters when the trees around them flashed so bright they turned blue. Just as Thor's eyes readjusted, thunder crashed earburstingly close. One, two, three. Three miles.

The storm was getting closer. Fast.

For Thor, the metaphor was so strong it was almost embarrassing. The storm was upon him, after days of circling, and he knew he now had a chance to use the storm to his advantage.

'Hey, Chesters,' Thor said, turning back to the policeman.

'What?' Chesters said, spreading his arms in exasperation. He'd had enough, and now felt he'd gone too far afield in more ways than one.

The late afternoon exploded around them in an earth-shattering jolt, a fierce bolt of lightning crashing at the exact same time as the thunder. The effect on the men was concussive and confusing—but one of them was ready for it.

Thor dove at Chesters, shoving him hard off his feet. Chesters fell back, flailing, into the water, his fall absorbed by the soft mud floor beneath the flow. The problem wasn't the impact though, it was the disorientation. He flailed wildly on the floor, while Thor sprinted off through the trees.

If nobody was going after Roisin, he'd have to go after her himself, broken wrist, ribs and all—and balls to the consequences. He'd gladly do whatever time was demanded as long as she was OK, and this godawful turn of events was over.

He tossed the jacket and ran through the rain. He knew from experience that the storm should have moved through a little by now, bustled along by the winds that landed icy punches on his soaked clothes.

White everywhere, so sudden again. Thor shielded his eyes and kept moving. Chesters shouted his name from somewhere behind him, but it was immediately engulfed by the crash of thunder. Four. The storm was quickly moving through, and would soon be gone. Thor abruptly changed direction, dropping right and ducking between a stand of quivering spruces. Through the stand was a thick holly bush, and feeling buzzed by fear, painkillers, and cold, hard adrenaline, he pushed straight into the heart of the bush.

The leaves nicked and jabbed at his face, poked claws into his sides, sought out any exposed slip of skin and bit hard, but he clamped his jaw tight. The deeper he pushcd, the easier it became, as the bush swallowed him whole. Engulfed, he heard the urgent splashing of footsteps getting closer.

'Fuck, fuck, fuck, fuck me, fuck…' babbled Chesters as he ran past.

He would likely be in for the biggest of rollockings for this.

Thor waited and waited, trying not to let his fears for what could be happening to Roisin consume him and make him blow his cover. Ten minutes went by, and those same splashing footsteps returned.

Slower. Beaten, retreating through the woods to the road and the waiting squad car. Chesters had given up.

Thor gave it another five, then forced himself out of the needled clutches of the holly. He acknowledged that no amount of earnest explanation would get him out of the serious trouble he knew his actions would bring. He was a fugitive now, but somehow the thought gave him backbone. Spine. It was him against the world now—and he was damned if he was going to let it beat him

36

'He's escaped. The police are so shit in this village. They literally don't know their elbow from their arse.'

The listener took a long minute to think. The disappointments of the last few days had left them too open to exposure. They had underestimated almost every hurdle to their plans. It would be easy to back out now, despite the obviousness of the rewards.

But this? This was a second chance. With Thor no longer in custody, the chances of his finally meeting that early grave were far higher.

'Are you still there?' asked the caller.

'Yes, I just can't talk now. How did you find out?'

'I just listened in to the call at Crook's Farm. Told Tilly Crook that he'd got away from the police and was most likely on his way back over there following the hunches he was hysterical about. Apparently.'

'So... we've got another bite of the cherry?' 'Yes.'

'You must admit this hasn't exactly gone to plan, has it?'

'The rewards will be worth it. One-point-two million pounds, split two ways. Think of that.'

'You need me for that. Whatever happens now, you need me for that share. Because this is going to ignite a war, and I need to remind you which side you are on.'

'Yeah, yeah, I know. Believe me, when I've got my share, you won't be hearing from me again.'

'I think that's a good idea. You are one rare breed that I'm not sure

is too great for my well-being.'

Despite the depth of their desires, both of them had found that trying their hand at breaking the law had been far from simple and easy.

'Is it raining your way?' 'What do you think?

37

Thor couldn't go to his family. The police would have them under their eye, and the same could be said for any of his acquaintances. So, alone, soaked yet driven, he continued up Hollow. The water was up to his shins now, so he walked up the bank to the drystone wall.

Crook's Farm was where he was going, against all semblance of sense, and as he hopped the dry wall to access the flatter fields at the top, he thought helplessly about how much had happened since he had made this walk only the previous night, or how much had happened since this time two nights ago, or even three.

Roisin would be there, this he believed, and Thor would be proved right. He had to believe it, and he clung to that with all the boldness in his heart. He had no wallet, no keys, no phone—all had been confiscated by Okpara.

He tried to think like a killer, to wrap his mind around the ugly parameters of a brain that was prepared to kill a person, and bend all truths to keep that killing hidden. What would this person be doing now? If the fall guy had escaped, and you knew that he knew you were guilty?

It didn't take Thor long to work it out: you'd move the body, and get the hell out.

Which meant he felt little surprise to see, on his approach to Crook's Farm, that the Crooks appeared to be moving house.

They had pulled a huge green John Deere tractor out in front of the farmhouse, and had attached a massive roofed trailer to the back of it, which had one tarp side lashed down and the other parted just enough to allow things to be stowed by Mason and the brothers.

Thor could only assume that this was not the behaviour of the innocent, but any confrontation with them would only delay his finding Roisin. He therefore decided to circumvent the property and take a wide arc around the zone in which he remembered the security lights fell. He'd have to be doubly careful, since Tilly Crook was riding shotgun, literally, in the cab of the tractor, peering out into the night with eagle eyes and that bloody huge twelve-gauge.

The house wasn't what Thor was after anyway, but the outbuildings. When he fell yesterday, as he made his way through the scrub, he had noted the buildings further back from the house. Thinking back to his hypothetical murderer's mind, he thought that'd be a good place to house a kidnapped person. And his travels the night before had shown him a pretty good route to get to them.

The ground around his feet was getting softer, signaling another change in the flood plain beneath his feet. The balance of the water table here was taking an almighty scrambling. His shoes were filling with water again. His progress was creating obvious splashing, so he kept his speed as tempered as he could.

Before the outbuildings was a yard, which was struggling, just as Pat Hurst had said—it was underwater, with the drains spitting fetid water up and out in three of the four corners of the yard.

The outbuildings comprised a group of stables and sheds bathed in darkness and the shit-smelling water. They looked so old, disused, and desperate that he couldn't possibly imagine that they would be used for any actual purpose these days. He knew for a fact that the main yard was where all the heavy lifting was done; this area was just a forgotten feature and footnote to a chapter in the farm's history, when livestock and horses were part of the day to day.

As he readied himself to plough into the muck, he heard a loud plop in the water next to him. It was as if something had fallen out of the tree. He looked up.

There was another one, distinctly. Yes, definitely.

He shielded his eyes. The tree above him was a green conifer, slick with rain. It didn't feel right.

A glint caught his eye. Higher than the treetop, but not by much.

Closer to the house, high up almost near the roof.

Movement. He caught it, just as his eyes had almost scanned clean across. The left-hand window, next to the one he leapt from last night. It was dark but open, and in the bottom part of the open frame he could see something bobbing in and out of view erratically. He stepped closer, but because of the angle, he couldn't see what was in the window.

Recognition flared at the same time as euphoria.

The bobbing object was the top of Roisin's head, and her eyes. She was looking down at him, unable to get any higher than her eyes above the ledge, and was probably too scared to shout out to him. She must have been throwing something out to catch his attention. Thor thanked God it had worked.

He was elated, and drowned drunk on love and purpose. She was up there. Roisin was alive. He would do anything to get to her. He quickly reviewed the obstacles separating them: the Crooks, two flights of stairs, the walls of the house itself.

A diversion was needed—urgently.

Thor cast about the back patio, which was beneath only three inches of water. Shattered pieces of patio furniture floated lazily on the surface, rain-drummed. The back of the house was dark, and the only visible access was a stable-style door in the centre.

He looked through the nearest windows, into darkness. He was peering into the kitchen, he could just about tell, but it had been cleaned out, the only thing left being a vast green Aga that looked more like a tugboat engine, and some old kitchen utensils still on wall hooks.

The Crooks were definitely leaving.

He ran back around the house, desperate to come up with an idea. If he could distract the Crooks, he could possibly get into the house via the stable door, and up the stairs to Roisin.

He edged around the corner of the front of the property with nothing more than an eyeball, and saw nobody. The trailer was still there, with the tarp now fully tied down. The cab of the tractor was empty. Thor looked at the cars but couldn't remember if there were the same number as when he'd arrived. The door of the house was open, spraying light out onto the porch step, catching silver arrows of rain.

But something was amiss. Where were the Crooks?

An icy tremor shook Thor's brainstem as he imagined them marching upstairs to finish off Roisin, the only piece of property that they didn't need anymore. He couldn't waste any time.

He edged into the quiet courtyard, up onto the porch, and ran inside.

Standing on the stairs across the hall, arranged almost as if in a team photo for a hunting squad, stood the Crook clan, rifles raised and trained on him.

Trapped.

Thor braced himself, waiting for the first explosion to rip through him and bring a new thunder to the night, but all he heard was the fierce slushing churn of wet gravel, the squeal of wet brakes, and the roar of an engine. Headlights threw spangles through the windows into the darkened rooms, and silhouetted Thor in the door frame. Another set of headlights followed. Thor held his breath.

All eyes left Thor, and Tilly broke the silence: 'Spread to the windows. It's time.' The Crook's disbanded into the adjoining rooms with near military precision.

Thor could only stand in blank confusion, but whatever threat had arrived, he didn't want to come between it and the Crooks. If it was the police, it was about time. It had to be the police, come for the Crooks at last. As soon as the stairs were empty, Thor ran for them, and didn't look back, taking them two at a time. He made it to the middle landing when a deep voice broke out—one that he wasn't expecting but still recognised instantly.

'You've ruined us, and now you are leaving,' shouted Wilkes Loxley Sr. 'I can do nothing about that, but if you have Thor and the young girl, now is the time to hand them over.'

Thor could only stand on the middle landing and listen, as things went decidedly Western in Crook's Hollow.

A cackle rang out from the bottom floor, followed by Tilly Crook's scratchy tones: 'The irony. The irony. Loxleys on our property, and we hold all the cards. We've waited years for this. Years.'

Thor took the next set of stairs at speed, and was faced with the same two grain loft doors as last night. He knew left was the man cave, so he chose right.

It was a storage room, full of all sorts of garbage that had been shoved higher and higher out of sight: couches, an old table, a bird cage, some canisters, old suitcases, a fish tank, a suit of armour with several pieces missing. Must and mildew hung thick in the air, but the breeze from the window was shifting it for what must have been the first time in ages. And under the window, bound to a radiator with lengths of blue rope, sat Roisin. She gasped when she saw him, and he ran over, picking his way through the piled objects.

Thor saw her clearly in the moonlight. The skin around her left eye was an angry purple, her lips bloodied and cracked. Her fingers were tipped with bloodied nails, where she had obviously tried to claw her way free. Her hair was slick with rainwater from the window, and blood trickled thinly from her scalp.

It was wet all around her, and Thor's nose pricked at the realisation it wasn't just rain.

'I'm sorry,' said Roisin, between thin, shallow sobs, her eyes so alive yet scared. Thor didn't know what she was apologising for, save for relieving herself, and, as his heart swelled with protection, he rushed to embrace her.

'I've got you sweetheart,' he said, cradling her. 'I've got you.' She sobbed against his shoulder. She was wearing the same clothes as she'd worn last night in her trailer. She had been tied up here since then.

A gunshot rang out from down below, startling them. Another followed, then soon after, another.

'We have to get out of here. Our families have gone to war,' said Thor, as he started to fumble at the ropes holding her to the radiator pipes.

'Where do we go?' said Roisin, trying to angle herself to help him free her. The ropes had been heavily knotted, and it took time to undo them. She rubbed her wrists as she stood shakily with Thor's help. 'Do you know a back way out?'

'Yes, follow me,' answered Roisin, as she stumbled through the jumble of the room.

The gunfire was sparse, but it persisted. A gunfight was ensuing below. They made it to the second floor, and waited for a second, looking over the banister to the bottom floor. When a gun was fired it was much louder here and each explosion cut through the house. They waited for a break in the action.

The next shot was more muffled, and had clearly come from outside, but in response, glass tinkled on stone, someone screamed, and a male voice shouted 'No!'

That was their cue, and Roisin led, taking Thor's hand. As they approached the entryway, one of the Crook brothers started crawling from the right-hand door across the hall towards the kitchen. He was holding his neck, and gasping, 'Mummy... Mummy.' Gunfire from the house erupted again, this time with much more regularity. The man on the floor was wide-eyed with terror and leaving a trail of thick red blood right across the floor.

Thor had never seen anything so visceral, and his stomach turned. Roisin turned and pulled him away from the hall, deeper into the house. Down a short corridor lined with empty coat pegs, they were at the back stable door. They quickly slid the deadbolts free, but froze for a moment as Tilly Crook screamed. It didn't sound like the scream of someone mortally wounded—it came out of a much worse pain. She had seen what happened to her son.

The gunfire stopped.

Thor and Roisin ran out into the night, off the back step and into the standing water at the back of the house, and ran towards the main drive and the cars.

As they rounded the house, engines started up again. Thor recognised one of them, the old green Land Rover Discovery. It drove up to them and braked sharply. The driver opened the door: Wilkes Sr. Wilkes Jr. was sat next to him in the front passenger seat.

'Thank God. Get in now,' Wilkes Sr. said. His hair was rain-swept

and wild, and his face was set in a combination of shock and grim determination. Thor and Roisin wasted no time and ran for the back seats, as another bloodcurdling scream from Tilly ripped through the rain.

They set off, and Thor stole a glance ahead. In the second car, which he recognised as Hollis's Jeep, sat three figures he guessed were Hollis, Crewe, and Mercy.

'You all came to get us?' Thor said, stunned.

'When the police said you had got away, we knew there was only one place you were going to go,' said Wilkes Sr. 'You were right. They had her. I can't believe it.'

Thor pulled Roisin close to him. She was shivering and silent. Dad isn't the only one going into shock, thought Thor.

'What happened back there?' Thor asked. Wilkes Jr. looked across at his father balefully.

'I shot him,' Wilkes Sr. said, in a voice barely audible over the pumping wiper blades. 'I shot him, and I think I may have killed him.' He glanced back at Thor in the rearview. There would be deep and severe consequences, and his eyes bore the weight of every single one of them.

38

The three-mile clip across Crook's Hollow usually took five or six minutes, tops. Tonight, this night of emptied heavens and small-town hells, it was a slow, painful crawl to the war-drum beat of torrential rain on the car roof. Through the windshield, as Hollis' more modern car pulled away smoothly into the black, water arrowed in the headlights like a soaked trip through warp speed in Star Wars.

'What happens now?' asked Thor.

'I don't know,' his father said. 'We'll see what morning brings.'

To Thor that sounded far too philosophical to be of any use. Wishing the night away wasn't going to bring the sun up any quicker.

'We need to see how the farm is,' Wilkes Jr. said, eyes fixed ahead. 'The well gone again?' asked Thor.

'Water everywhere,' replied his brother. 'The well was gushing out, and the yard was underwater. That was when we got the call and left. Christ knows what's happening now.'

'Where's Mum and Rue? Where are the kids?'

'Mine are at home. Seems OK out there. Rue's is underwater. She's stuck in Windle Heath in standstill traffic. Barry's out on the roads, if you can believe that on a night like this, so the kids are upstairs at the farm with Mum.'

'They could be trapped by now,' Thor said. 'Yep, they could.'

Thor felt Roisin's thumb on the back of his hand, rubbing back and forth softly. He leant against her and kissed her hair. She smelt of that shampoo he loved, but with an overlay of grit and grime. He couldn't have cared less. He felt rather than saw his father's hackles raise, as he shifted in his seat, but Thor preempted his protest.

'Don't Dad. Just don't.'

Thor could see his father's hands flexing on the steering wheel. It was amazing how blood could still boil at such pointless history as Roisin's lineage, that even now something so simple and genuinely innocent could fire up old angst like a classic car kept perfect but never used.

As Wilkes Sr. opened his mouth to say something, a mighty impact shook the car on its axles, causing the rear end to tailspin. The occupants fell across each other, seat belts having been forgotten in favour of a hasty escape. Thor thought they must have hit a pothole, or maybe a deer. You couldn't see anything in this weather. The car ran into a hedgerow, front end dipping slightly as it entered.

'Christ!' shouted Wilkes Sr.

Thor righted himself in the back. 'You OK?' asked Roisin. Thor would have nodded, but over her head, out of the window, smudged into an ugly watercolour by droplets, he could see a car pull up. The headlights were off and Thor had a very bad feeling.

'Go. Go. GO!' he shouted.

Wilkes Sr. turned to see what Thor was looking at.

'Go, Dad, now!' bellowed Thor, as a figure got out of the car and walked towards the Discovery. Wilkes Sr. suddenly grasped the situation and reached for the gear stick, slamming it in reverse. The car juddered backwards, hopping out of the hedge, when another all too familiar explosion blasted deafeningly close. The driver's side window shattered, revealing Ward Crook, shotgun smoking and raised, soaked to the skin with hate etched on his features. Evil lit his eyes, and he raised the gun again.

Thor and Wilkes Jr. both screamed for him to stop, but another blast and Wilkes Sr. jolted violently in his seat. Blood splashed the beige dashboard of the Discovery.

Wilkes Jr. screamed but Thor couldn't hear it—the blasts had deafened him temporarily.

Ward lowered the shotgun and took a long look at the car. A veil seemed to hang in front of him. It was impossible to know what he was thinking, but clearly something had been done that for all the world could never be undone. Without a word, Ward got back in his car, started it, and drove away.

Thor pulled himself forward between the two front seats. 'Who's hit?' he shouted, but Wilkes Jr. was already leaning over his father, answering the question. Thor looked at his father, who was slumped in the seat. The blood on the dashboard and wheel was arced in thin splatters, and the front of Wilkes

Sr.'s jacket was a shred of dark fabric, torn pink flesh and deep red blood, welling slowly in the shallow cavity. The grim, unburnished reality of what man is made of hit Thor hard.

'Dad!' Wilkes Jr. cried, reaching for the wound with a stuttering hand but not having a clue on earth what to do about it. He put his hand on his father's shoulder, and his features cracked in grief. He knew, from a farming life of bitter dirt and blood and life and death, that this was it. This is one you don't get up from.

Wilkes Sr.'s head slumped against the door frame, filling the gaping hole where the window should have been, and rain fell on his head and into his eyes.

Thor crawled past Roisin, who was now curled in the footwell quietly sobbing, and got out of the car. He went to his father and put his hand on his cheek. He was deathly pale but with a pink blush on his cheeks that looked strangely like stage makeup, but was only the rain diluting the blood that had splashed there.

The old man's eyes creaked open, and a word dropped from his lips. It was Thor's name, and for the first and last time, he called Thor by how he wanted to be known and not by how he was christened.

'Yes, Dad,' Thor said, his eyes full of hot tears. He leaned in close, his father's breath soft yet stale in his face.

'The safe. Please. Twenty-one, twenty-two, nineteen.' 'Yes, I'll go.'

Wilkes Sr. gave a slight nod.

'I love you, Dad,' said Thor, 'and I'm so sorry. I'm so sorry.'

Wilkes Jr. was crying, his face buried in his father's jacket. There was blood on his face too. Thor could do nothing but hold his father while the old man passed away in the rain, and Thor imagined that the heavens would stay open long enough for his father to pass through their gates.

39

They found a picnic blanket in the boot of the Discovery, covered in dog hair, but it was the best they could do. Wilkes Jr. split the seats down the back and he and Thor lay their father there, covered by the blanket.

Wilkes Jr. sat behind the wheel, but getting his father's blood on his hands proved too much for him, and he hadn't even got the car in gear before he was a stuttering wreck again. Roisin was still huddled in the remaining back seat, shocked and unresponsive, her strength overtaxed.

Thor took over, and edged the nose of the Land Rover slowly out of the hedge, bringing brambles with it that had got caught in the grille. When he was a kid he'd often dreamt of driving this car—his dad's car. And now finally behind the wheel he came to two realisations, first, it was bloody smooth and light in its responsiveness, and second, he didn't want it anymore. Not after what had happened, and what he'd just seen.

He knew it would take a long time to come to terms with recent events, especially the plain awfulness of the last few moments, but he'd have to file that for later. This was all-out war now. Loxley versus Crook.

'We have to kill them. We have to kill them all,' muttered Wilkes Jr. between sobs.

Thor was keenly aware that his brother was talking about murdering Roisin's family—he hoped he didn't mean her too. He just wanted to turn the whole thing over to the police. Thor himself was a fugitive, and now a murder had been committed. Any action by the Loxleys now would contribute to their own destruction.

The next moments became a string of snapshots that Thor would come across from time to time—painful pictures accidentally scattered on an attic floor while you look for something else:

—The lights of Loxley Farm in the distance, and the dreadful news they were bringing…

—Pulling into the yard in a foot of brown water, seeing yet more water flooding out of the front door of the farmhouse…

—The children's faces in the upstairs windows peering out in confusion and wonder…

—Seeing Wilkes Jr. fall to his knees in the flood, and Hollis, Crewe, and Mercy running to him…

—The look on their faces as he told them, the way they looked at the Discovery as if disbelieving what they saw…

—The awful anguished crying that followed…

—Bunny Loxley screaming from the second floor as the news was taken up, her hands on her head…

Thor looked back at the outline of his father in the back. How huge the man looked in death beneath his improvised shroud.

The safe. Thor had fucked up so much between himself and his father. He owed his father. His last request must stand. The safe.

'Roisin,' he said. 'Sweetheart, come here.'

Roisin looked up at him slowly. Her gaze was passive, her features slack.

'I need to go in, darling, OK?'

Her breathing was shallow as a sparrow's. But she nodded, and after a moment's hesitation she opened the passenger door with a quivering hand.

They started walking over to the house when Mercy, mad with grief and rage, marched up to them.

'You bring her here? You bring her here!' She poked the barrel of a short shotgun he'd never seen before almost right under Roisin's chin.

'I'm sorry,' Roisin said, but Thor got between them. 'She's innocent,' Thor said. 'They had kidnapped her.'

'I don't give a flying shit,' spat Mercy. 'No Crook has any right here.

Not now. Not ever. Not after what they've done.'

Thor pushed the barrel away. 'Mercy, please. She's innocent. You need to take care of Dad. He's still in the car.'

Mercy looked at the Discovery in bewilderment.

'God in heaven,' she whispered, as she started trudging slowly towards the car. The brothers took her lead and followed. Thor looked at the windows upstairs but could see nobody. The flood waters would never rise high enough to be a risk to those upstairs. The kids would be fine until morning; they'd have to be, because Thor had no idea how to get them out if things got worse.

'Wait here,' he said to Roisin. 'I'll be right back, I promise. Then we'll be away, OK? Get you warm.' He kissed her.

'I'm so sorry, Thor—about your dad,' she whispered.

They were both drenched now, rivulets pouring spouts off whatever angles they could find.

'Whatever anyone says about it, whatever they think, it was never your fault. Never once,' Thor said. He held her tight and whispered again, 'Never once.'

'I'll be right back, OK?' he said, as he gave her one last kiss. 'Find shelter,' he shouted as he ran to the house. He'd only just got her back and now he had to let her go again, a forced circumstance he fought against. But his Dad…. There was nothing else for it. If there was any wish of his father's he should try to execute, he should at least have a go at his dying one.

It took a hurdle over white water, to get over the front step and it was so angry, jutted and frothed by the two steps up and one back down, that he could have surfed it straight back to Roisin. In the kitchen he was shocked to see how bad things had gotten— two or three times worse than yesterday. Now, it was nearly waist deep and churning, a geyser.

He passed as quickly as he could through the kitchen and into the hall, but that still was up to his knees. He wondered if he could even get at the safe, let alone open it.

It was the disaster he expected. The surface of the flood water was

a gently rolling carpet of old paperwork. The desk still stood proud, the contents of the table top still exactly how they had been left, completely at odds with what was happening below it. Something humped, with sleek black fur, bobbed in the water by the desk. At first Thor thought it was an otter, but then he knew: Ruby. He'd been forgotten again, poor bastard.

Strangely, it was the biggest sign yet to Thor that things had properly gone to shit.

He didn't dwell on it. The safe was a huge, cumbersome brute that was so much a part of the furniture at Crook's Farm it would probably have a shout at the estate in probate now that Wilkes Sr. had passed. It was next to the filing cabinet in plain view, its combination wheel just a few inches above the waterline.

Twenty-one, twenty-two, nineteen.

Thor took the dial and spun, hearing the catches work their magic like he remembered from childhood.

A light snap and he pulled the door open with effort. A thick wad of drowned paperwork dislodged and presented itself. The safe stood five feet high, with a shelf marking every foot, so only the last two shelves were above water. Thor was hugely relieved to see that his father had still retained a modicum of common sense: on the top shelf, above the water, was a white, three-fold envelope, and written on it: THOR. It touched him again, his father writing his name how he preferred it.

He grabbed it, and he saw that underneath his name were three bullet points, etched in the same block-capital scratching:

·THE DEED
·THE TRUTH
·YOUR WILL

So much of that threw Thor a curveball he could never hope to read.

The Deed. The deed to his land. A church bell clanged in his head: the break-in at his flat above the post office. This must have been what they were after, it had to be. Thor had completely forgotten about it, more preoccupied with the impact of the scenario than its physical implications.

The Truth. Thor had no idea what that meant. None at all. He couldn't believe his father had anything to do with all the shit that had gone on in the last few days, so, barring some kind of huge about-face betrayal, Thor was stumped.

Your Will. This one troubled Thor most, for one main reason: he had never written one. He was twenty-five years old. What twenty-five- year-old writes a will? Not this one.

So this will had to be some kind of fake. And how in God's name had it ended up in the family safe?

The water sloshed over Thor's belt buckle, as he took the envelope. He couldn't work out whether to take it someplace else to open it and pore over its contents in peace, or...

With a trembling finger, he tore it open.

40

Numb, Thor emerged from the front doorway, a supermarket carrier bag under his arm.

The scenes both in front of him and lighting his imagination no longer registered. Roisin, the love of his life, elated to see him return. His siblings huddled around the open rear door of the Land Rover, paying their respects to their dead father. The Crooks, presumably brooding somewhere, waiting for the chance to finish them all off. The police, looking for him. Thor's nieces, nephews, sister, and mother stranded in the upper floors of the farmhouse, flood water rising. And all around them, the worst flood in the history of northern England, doing its best to sink, drown, wash away all memory and remnant of what had happened here.

'The kids and mum,' he shouted to his siblings, who looked over with weak expressions. They had had a little time with their father, the grim reality of his passing having clearly resonated. 'You should probably think about getting them.'

They jogged over through the bog that was the yard, Crewe arriving first. He looked relieved not to be staring at their father's corpse anymore, and seemed to be up for the task. 'You think it's getting worse in there?' he asked.

'That well isn't slowing down, and God knows when this water will stop. Best get them out. Between yourselves, you'll have them out of there in no time.'

'Where are you going?' asked Mercy with that indignant flash that made a mockery of her own name.

'I've got to get to the police. They'll be looking for me anyway. Take this, it's as much as I could grab from the safe.'

He handed the carrier bag to Crewe. 'And her?' Mercy was pointing at Roisin.

'She needs protective custody,' he said. Roisin looked like Thor had just spoken in backwards Latin, her eyebrows rising in confusion.

'What about Dad?' asked Hollis, to nobody in particular.

'I just… don't know. You'll think of something,' said Thor. 'Crewe, can I borrow your car?'

With a vacant look, Crewe handed keys to Thor.

'Just fucking like you, Thor, always creating the mess and leaving us to fix it,' Mercy spat.

'Oh, piss off. Piss right off,' said Thor as he marched to Crewe's Jeep. 'Roisin, come on, let's go.'

As she jogged over to follow him, she tried to grab his hand, and it was a gesture that hurt so much, so very much. He didn't know what she knew, and couldn't hurt her anymore—not after everything that had happened. He just didn't know how to act after what his father had left for him in the safe. His hand was limp around hers.

'What's the matter?' she asked. 'Did you get to the safe? Did you get what your dad told you to get?'

'Everything will be fine,' he said, as much to himself as her. 'I promise, it will all be OK.'

He said it, but he didn't know why. Like one of those things you say to frightened children: 'It'll be fine,' when in fact you've got no idea what the outcome will be. All you can do, when your own mind is asking panicky questions, is soothe those around you who need support.

The problem was, Thor knew everything was definitely not fine, definitely not OK—nor would it ever be.

41

They zipped along at a frantic rate, spraying water up the hedgerows. Roisin looked through the windshield between her fingers, unnerved at the speed.

'Thor, please, I understand if you don't want to talk but where are we going?' she said. 'I'm scared, Thor. Really scared.'

'Protective custody is what I said, and I'm afraid it's exactly what I meant,' Thor replied, softly. There were so many reasons why protective custody was the right thing for Roisin now, but the biggest was clearly that there were more pressing matters—and he needed to put concerns about Roisin's safety to bed for a while so he could go and address it.

The truth was that, thanks to his father's little care package, Thor now had a fair idea of someone who had a very good reason for wanting him dead. Someone he hadn't thought of, or dared imagine. And he had to get to the bottom of it.

'But if you go anywhere near a police station, you'll be arrested straight away,' Roisin said.

'That's why I need you to go and hand yourself in. You can't go back to Crook's Farm, not after what they did to you, and that includes your caravan, because they'll come looking for you there too. I'll drop you off at the station in Windle Heath, but you'll have to go in alone. I'm so sorry that it has to be like that.'

Roisin was hushed by his words. 'You're scaring me, Thor. Baby, what are you going to do?'

Thor couldn't answer. 'It'll be OK,' was all he could muster.

'Seeing your Dad like that…' she tried to begin, acknowledging the scale not only of what they had been through in the last few days, but the sheer blunt fact that Thor had watched his father's murder. Thor knew the sudden death of a family member is lain thick with horror at the best of times, but actually being there for it is something you wouldn't wish on your worst enemy—and it seemed that this was something that Roisin herself was beginning to grasp.

It was something that would hold them together forever, witnessing that, amongst everything else.

From the high ground of the two farms, water surged downhill towards Crook's Hollow. This was reflected in the roads, which now looked more like swift, narrow rivers heading downstream apace. Crewe's Jeep handled the conditions well, considering the water, the mud, and the terrain.

Before long, they were on Main Street, greeted by scenes from a low-budget disaster film. It was the end of days in little England. Water flushed down the gradual incline of Main Street, flooding right up to porches and doorways, but anything close to the streets was in two to three feet of water. The retirement residences, with their tight windows to the street and front doors that once kicked you straight to the curb, looked like a shitty Venice.

In the flatter parts of the road, the water had that thickness to it, that languid laziness of movement that suggested it was going nowhere fast. This would take ages to shift. The water table in this area would be forever altered, and because of that, Clyne's master plan might no longer be relevant. It might already be dead in the water, so to speak.

Thor hoped it wasn't yet. He needed it. To flush out his enemies, he needed his land to still retain its value.

The water reached all the way to the high wheel arches of the Jeep, which trundled steady. Huge clumps of hay coasted lazily downstream of this new river from the small stud farm a couple of streets along. The streetlights cast the whole waterway an eerie warm lemon glow; there was still power, but that would bring its own set of problems.

Thor had expected to see residents scrambling to save their possessions before the flood consumed everything. But Crook's Hollow was fast becoming a sub-aquatic ghost town. Roisin's jaw was limp and hanging, but it seemed to Thor like nothing would shock him anymore. There must have been an evacuation alert earlier, and the residents had done as they were told.

He moved the Jeep through Crook's Hollow, experience guiding the car on a road he couldn't see, and before long they were out on the A-road connecting Crook's Hollow to Windle Heath, two miles away. Once on the main road, the water suddenly stopped at a bend, where runoff from higher fields was sieving through a thick hedge. Thor pulled the Jeep from the water as if he was driving up a dock, past a police roadblock with his head down.

'I'm not sure anything will ever be the same again,' said Roisin. 'That was hundreds of thousands of pounds worth of damage. The village... it's all gone to pieces.' She reached for him, placing her palm on the back of his hand on the gear stick. To Thor, her touch felt different. His affection for her was massive, but its fundamental pillar was altered forever.

Before long, they arrived, exhausted, in Windle Heath. Thor would have given anything for a bed—a bed and some time to get his head straight. Windle Heath was different from Crook's Hollow in a lot of ways, but the biggest one tonight was that it was not underwater. The rain was falling, but the drainage system here seemed to be holding firm.

The police station was in the middle of the village, and it took Thor no time at all to reach it. The residents had apparently listened to the warnings of the evacuation in the next village and were staying inside, awaiting word on what was to come next. The village looked like a settlement in wartime: empty streets, with lonely lights on in windows, people using as little power as possible.

Windle Heath was laid out in a Y shape, with a main road that entered to the south which split north-east and north-west respectively, on an island over which watched the village Sainsbury's. When the old provision store was bought by the corporate retail behemoth, many residents thought it would be the end of Windle Heath as it was. Thor remembered the time well: provision stores were the kind of places where everybody knew who you were and the butchers at the back of the shop used to keep particular cuts of meat behind for most villagers, not because they asked or ordered, but simply because they were known and remembered. Now, the idle aisles of Sainsbury's certainly knew who you were, especially if you were that week's gossip. Thor hated the place for what it was and its affordable convenience. He was, like everybody else, a begrudging regular.

They came down the top left fork of the Y, turned left at the roundabout, and back up the right fork. They didn't see another car or soul the whole time. Moreover, the bars and restaurants which frosted either side of the Y joint like underarm hair were all shut, and a journey which would normally have been doused in soft neons and muffled laughter beyond the glass was absent.

At the station, Thor pulled up in one of the many empty bays. It was quiet.

'I'll be back soon. I promise,' he said.

'You're sure this is the right thing to do?' Roisin asked. She sat upright in her seat, looking at Thor pleadingly.

'It has to be,' said Thor, looking at the front door of the station house. There was a reception inside behind automatic glass doors, and it looked to be unmanned. He wondered if anyone was in the station house at all. 'I don't know what I'm doing, but I need to know you're going to be safe, OK?'

'I understand that. I just don't understand why I can't be with you.' 'There are things I've got to do. Like I said. There's only so many ways out of this for us all, and I need to find at least one of them.' 'Do you have any ideas?'

'Yes.'

It was partly the truth. He had something in mind. Something that would bring the moth to the flame.

Roisin looked uncertain. 'I trust you,' she said finally. 'But make sure you come back to me. Do you understand that?'

'I do.'

'Do you love me? You better had.' She tried to smile weakly.

'Yes, I do. I will always,' he said. He took her hand and squeezed it. 'You have to go, now, before someone sees me.'

Roisin blew a kiss and ran across the tarmac toward the cold glow of the station. Thor wasted no time, reversing back out into the street without paying any heed to the traffic—not that there was any. As he drove back towards the roundabout, his mind wound tight around itself like a boa constrictor. It was rooted in what he had to do now, the trap he had to lay, and the weight of what he'd learned when he opened the envelope his father had left for him…

In his father's office, Thor had sat on the battered desk chair, a dead dog occasionally floating against his thighs, in flood water that rose six full inches in that time. He'd felt as if his moorings had come adrift, as if he was an oil rig way out to sea, and his foundation struts had cracked irreparably under a seismic shift.

In fact, seismic wasn't grand enough to describe how much things

had changed in light of what he had read. This was a galactic

alteration to the landscape. His landscape.

He felt such a fool, such an idiot. The air in the office was suffocating. He began to hate it all—this room, especially—and hate its connection to the man who usually used it. His father.

The bastard had betrayed him. The bastard had betrayed them all.

And now he was dead—he'd got away with it. The hurt he left behind would be huge, and he'd never have to deal with it.

Thor wondered if anyone else knew. If anyone had ever twigged, unlike thick old Thor, whose every action had only worked to unknowingly make things worse.

All the things he had done, which he wouldn't have done if he had known.

The whole experience was hollowing out a deep and abiding cynicism inside him, one that he would likely retain the rest of his days. However, it was that cynicism that he needed to embrace to flip the situation on its head and catch the perpetrators once and for all: it was breeding in him the tools for a trap.

The envelope was secreted in his jacket pocket. The envelope contained, among other things, the deeds to the portion of land he

owned. He was prepared to bet anything on those deeds being the reason for the break-in at his flat, and that told him something important: that his adversaries had a fall back plan. They must have thought that even if Thor didn't die, they could still get the land somehow, and the deed was somehow crucial to that.

He wished he knew more about the legal process behind it, but it didn't matter – the deed had attracted his adversaries before, and would do again. He could use it as bait.

Thor knew the main road in to Crook's Hollow was blocked, so he turned off a mile from the roadblock at Windle Heath Golf Club. He knew the access routes used by the landscape buggies, having used them to walk back from the Heath to Loxley Farm many times. He could use them as a cut through.

The single-track roads were in a disarray of mud and tumbling water, and it took Thor half an hour of gentle persuasion to get the Jeep into Crook's Hollow. He arrived at the Traveller's Rest, parked the Jeep at the back of the car park, and made it inside to hear the bell for last orders sound brightly.

When Thor burst in, Martin Campbell had rung the bell for, it seemed, precisely nobody. The lights were on, the fridges humming, but the pub's floor was swimming in a healthy six inches of water. Thor saw Pat Hurst perched on a bar stool with two pints being placed in front of him next to the two he already had. His toes were dangling up above the water, and somehow his shoes were dry. The pub had flooded around the gnarly boozer.

'Ye jus' made it for 't end u'days,' muttered Pat.

Thor didn't argue—even with the slurring, Pat was making good sense.

'Martin, please, I need a favour,' Thor shouted over the counter into the back of the pub, but when Martin came in Thor immediately regretted it. Martin looked ravaged and beaten, completely destroyed. Bags dragged his eyes into purple hollows, his arms were filthy, and his brow was caked in sweat and mud.

'That bad, huh?' said Thor.

'I've spent the whole day bailing out a cellar that was only to

collapse a couple of hours ago. The water just won't… I'm ruined, Thor. Ruined. The pub is gone.'

'What do you mean gone? You're insured, right?'

Martin laughed loudly, a humourless cackle that echoed in the empty pub.

'I gambled. They said this was a flood plain, and that a building like this would be uninsurable. Can you believe that? So I looked at public records for floods. Nothing since 1504. Fifteen-oh-bloody-four. So I didn't bother, thought I'd save the cash.'

Thor understood. Unless he had a hundred thousand quid stashed somewhere for exactly this occurrence, he and the pub were both buggered.

'I'm so sorry, mate,' said Thor. 'This is probably the worst timing ever, but are the phones still working? And if they are, can I please make a quick call?'

Martin's mind was still elsewhere, and he simply waved Thor to the back of the bar. Thor went back, picked up the receiver and dialed Loxley Farm. It was time to chum the waters.

He knew where the phone points around the farm were, and he knew they'd put a line out into the main barn, so his father could conduct the odd bit of business on the hoof, and not have to take all his gear off to answer calls. This was before mobile phones of course, but Thor knew it was still there last time he'd checked, and now he could picture the sound of the phone ringing out across the yard. He felt sure that's where they'd have gone when the kids had been pulled out of the house, it being the nearest point of shelter.

The line was abruptly picked up. 'Yeah?' said an abrupt tense voice. 'Hollis, is that you?'

'Yeah, Thor what do you want? We are kind of busy here, in case you forgot.'

'I know, I'm sorry. Listen, I need to ask you something, could you just put the word across the family that I've forgotten something at The Traveller's Rest. It's my deed from the safe. I'd just stopped in to pick up a couple of bits and must have dropped the envelope. Martin's holding it behind the bar, so, yeah, if you could just pass it on that next

time anyone's passing, could they pick it up for me? Thanks.'

'OK, I'll do that, but I can't picture anyone being able to get there for a while.'

'That's fine, no rush. I appreciate it.'

Thor hung up. He knew that as soon as word got around that the envelope containing the deeds was behind the bar, his adversaries wouldn't be able to resist just strolling over and picking them up. All Thor had to do was wait to see who would walk in the door.

The more he thought about it though, the more he felt he could really upset the apple cart. He looked up into the recesses behind the bar, at the CCTV cameras. He knew they were all wired only for video and not audio, but they would serve as a decent record of who came in and roughly what went down.

With that in mind, he picked up the receiver again. There was one more person he wanted to invite.

42

The caller was thrilled with the news. After the monumental fuck-ups of the last few days, the arrests and now the deaths, they were getting somewhere. Get to the pub, get the deed, get the cash.

They felt they deserved a bit of fortune. Thor had proven far trickier than expected. He was so difficult to pin down, and so lucky, too, the bastard. Who knew that all this would have to go down at the same time as the worst flooding the region had ever seen?

'So get to the pub, and it's job done. Doesn't matter where he is, as long as we have the deeds we can work from there. They can't be that hard to change,' the caller said.

'I don't want to be seen going into the pub, though.'

'You'll have to. Besides, he asked for someone to go and get them. In a way we are only doing what we were asked to do. And as soon as we have those deeds, we'll be out of here. And I can't wait to leave this godawful place behind.'

'You sure? You're sure this is the right thing to do now?'

'Thor doesn't know shit. He hadn't even seen the deed before today, and he even left them in the pub. He obviously hasn't got a clue. Get them so we can get out of here.'

'I still think killing him is the way to go.'

'Well, forgive me, but you've had quite a few goes at that already and it's not quite gone to plan, has it?'

The other choked back a retort, and imagined the roles reversed. It was no fun trying to kill someone when you'd never done it before.

'Where are you now?' asked the caller.

'About two minutes away. The street is slow, shall we say.' 'When you've got it, let me know. I'll meet you where we said.'

'OK. It'll probably be in about five minutes. I'm not going to hang about. The pub's just up ahead now.'

43

Thor had hurried back to one of the booths facing the bar, and sat out of sight from the door. Whoever came in wouldn't see him and spook, they'd have to really show themselves to the cameras well before sprinting off. But it all depended on who arrived first.

Pat Hurst only had one pint left by the time the outer door to the pub clunked, water splashed, and the opening inner door birthed ripples that blossomed across to the bar.

Whoever had opened it came in with long, noisy strides, and as he got to the bar, Thor finally saw who it was. His tormentor, unmasked at last.

'I heard you were working on the roads,' said Thor.

The figure froze, then turned slowly to Thor. His features were as unremarkable as ever. Short dark hair flecked with platinum over sunken eyes. Certainly tall and broad enough to kill another man with just his hands.

Rue's husband, Barry.

'I was,' he said, turning to face Thor. 'But it'd been a hell of a day and I thought I'd have a quick pint on my way through. What are you doing here? Heard it's a bit of a mess up at the farm.' His manner was cold and he seemed to pick his words carefully.

'Bloody hell, you're good. You need to get your story straight, but I'd never have seen it.'

'What do you mean?' asked Barry, slowly edging to the booth, maintaining strong eye contact with Thor.

Barry and Thor had never really had a sit-down conversation, to the best of Thor's knowledge. He had been omnipresent for years, of course, and had been his sister Rue's only serious boyfriend right from the beginning. Classmates at the village school, they fell into their relationship seemingly out of nothing more magical than convenience, and he had drifted into their lives with the quiet nervous demeanour of a boy who was aware that the girl he was dating had three big brothers and a father not to be messed with. He had kept his own counsel for as long as Thor had known him, and Thor had foolishly assumed Barry wasn't the sharpest tool in the shed. But now he could see the calculation swirling behind those icy eyes.

'I mean you're bloody good. Do you know how I knew it was you?' Barry spread his hands as if trying to soothe Thor.

'Thor, I don't know what you're talking about. I got word to pick something up from the pub for you, while I was passing. I decided I'd stop for a quick one on my way through and get it for you. They said that things had gone mad up at the farm, and they'd tell me when I got there.'

'Yes, you stick to that. I know you're here to pick up the deed and you're hoping that that ridiculous will is with it. After all, it's the one bit of evidence that really ties you to what's been happening to me, isn't it? But you do know I've never written one, don't you? So me seeing one in my name might strike me as a little odd, wouldn't it?'

The corners of Barry's eyes creased almost imperceptibly, a tell so small yet as concrete as anything more dramatic. Thor pressed on.

'The thing is, the will itself is almost perfect. It fooled Dad. The one person I've not had a falling-out with at home, the one person I'm closest to out of all of them, the one who pretty much raised me... It

343

stands to reason I would leave it all to Rue, doesn't it?'

Barry slid into the booth opposite Thor.

'I'd be very careful saying things like that, Thor.'

'Or what? You'll make another shoddy attempt at trying to kill me, will you? I'll take my chances—you've done a real stand-up job of it so far. And the deed. You thought you could just edit it?'

Barry's stone-faced reaction spoke more eloquently than a denial would have done.

'You need a notary, witnesses—it needs a legal process. You can't just have them and rewrite them,' said Thor. 'And as for the will, well, you needed me dead, didn't you? Because with the will reading I leave everything I own to my sister Rue Turner, that would rather benefit you, wouldn't it? Four kids must be expensive… and you wanted me dead so that Rue could inherit my land, then you could persuade her to sell and get rich.'

The pub door clunked open and, right on cue, in walked Thor's second guest.

'You weren't joking, Mr. Loxley. This place has gone to shit. Do you know how hard it is to buy

344

Wellies at this time of night? Thank Christ for twenty-four-hour supermarkets,' said Lionel Clyne. He was wearing a grey pinstripe suit with an open-necked white shirt and the biggest pair of green Wellies Thor had ever seen. He looked—and smelled— pristine. Something musky.

'Lionel, thank you for coming,' said Thor.

'It's no problem at all. The blackjack tables in Manchester were getting cold, and the sniff of real money will always see me come running.'

'Lionel, I believe you've met Mr. Turner. He's the one who sounded you out about the value of the land.'

Clyne sat down next to Thor and looked at Barry.

'I'm sorry, Mr. Loxley, I can't say I have. He an advisor for you on the deal? I assume you called me here to accept in person?'

Thor was stumped. 'No—look at him. He asked you what the land was worth, didn't he? I bet it felt good, knowing you had a buyer once I'd snuffed it.'

Clyne, for the first time since Thor had known him, looked confused.

'Mr. Loxley, I don't know what you are suggesting but I don't like it. I made you that offer on good faith, I even gave you the cheque. Yes, there have been discussions with certain parties about potential offers for the land in question, but once it became apparent that it was yours and yours alone, I dealt with you directly. And I certainly have never met this man before.'

Thor's head swam. If Barry didn't know how much the land was worth, nor that an offer was likely to be made to buy it, then who told him? The first attempt on Thor's life came the night before anything regarding the development plan had been made public, so if Barry knew it was such a sought-after piece of land demanding a high price, how did he find out?

'Who did you sound out? Who came to you?' Thor asked Clyne, not sure he wanted to know the answer.

'A blonde girl. Youngish. Stout lady, if I remember right. She had balls on her. She already knew, though. She came to me.'

Thor's heart shivered as he felt the net drawing tighter. A knife of betrayal had been slowly working its way between his already broken ribs since he read the contents of the envelope, and it was plunging ever deeper.

'Where does this leave our deal, Mr Loxley?' asked Clyne. 'I assume I'm not out here for nothing.'

'You still want the land? With all this damage, you still want it?' Clyne laughed and splashed his feet playfully.

'Of course I do! Forgive me for bulldozing your naiveté, but this isn't the first shitty piece of land I'll turn for a profit and it won't be the last. One man's garbage is another man's treasure. The land is shite, utter shite, but to the council bigwigs, it's the goose that laid the golden egg. They had nowhere to put a major development until we greased the local wheels. We'll build it, they'll fulfil quotas, get government incentives, then we sell up and move on. It's the way the world works these days.'

'You're not getting it from me. This bastard wants it so he can sell it to you. Him and his fucking wife.'

As Thor gave voice to the names of those betraying him, his despair was complete. Rue, his sister, the woman who had raised him, and her husband, had tried to kill him so that in death, a fraudulent will would see Rue inherit Thor's piece of land, and she could sell it to Clyne and COMUDEV to make a fortune. Rue and Barry must have made the fake will, snuck it into the safe, and Wilkes Sr. must have thought it was genuine and put it in that damn envelope so it found its way back to Thor.

The pub phone rang, its bells filling the quiet, nearly empty room.

The three men looked at each other. The booth suddenly felt very small. The phone rang again, then Martin shouted into the pub. 'Thor? It's for you.'

Thor had Barry bang to rights, or as close to it. He couldn't let him out of his sight now he had him. Barry was staring at Thor, daring him to move with the eyes of a devilish lizard.

'Take a message for me,' Thor shouted.

'It's Roisin Crook... She sounds in a bad way.'

Roisin, again. Poor Roisin targeted for him. Thor couldn't stand the idea of her being hurt. Not again. He'd only just rescued her. But who had her? Not the police? Not Rue, surely?

'Ask her where she is,' replied Thor.

Campbell chattered urgently into the phone, then listened with a brow that furrowed deeper with each second.

'The caravan. She says Ward has gone mad, holding her prisoner there. He wants to see you, Thor, and no one else. Wait a minute… Christ… He says he wants you or she's dead.' He took the phone away from his ear. 'What the bloody hell is happening up there?'

Thor sprang up. 'Tell her I'll be right there.'

In the same instant, Barry leapt up and grabbed Clyne across the booth's table and viciously smashed his face on the table top with a vile crunch of nose cartilage on lacquered wood. Turner slid out of the booth, pulling Clyne with him by the neck.

'Give me the envelope, Thor, now. Or there'll be another death on your conscience.'

Thor looked at Barry in shock, still unable to grasp the fact that his sister's husband had these hidden, brutal depths, but Barry made things very real by pulling out a small, curved hand scythe and holding it to Clyne's throat. Clyne was barely conscious and blood was pouring from his broken nose. The blade fit perfectly around Clyne's neck, so well that it would take practically no effort at all to give him a brand new smile right under his chin.

'Tell her I'll be right there,' Thor said again, and Campbell, shocked, did just that. Pat Hurst had only just managed to turn around from the bar, and was staring at the scene in open-mouthed horror.

'You know he can't do a deal with you if you kill him,' Thor said. 'Money talks. Isn't that right, Clyne? he shouted. 'Your colleagues

would still go through with it. And if I don't kill you, you'll still accept, because this deal is worth that much, isn't it? But none of this is going to happen, because Thor is going to give me the envelope, you lot are going to keep your mouths shut, and we all get on with things. And Thor, if you ever say anything, ever breathe a word to anyone, I'll send you Roisin's intestines one slick foot at a time. That's how this goes from here.'

'What can you possibly do with it? The deed is signed in my name, for Christ's sake!'

Holding Clyne in place with the blade, Barry pulled a dog-eared bit of paper from his jacket. 'You get to stay alive, that little Crook bitch gets to stay alive, if you give me that envelope and keep your mouth shut – and that goes for everyone in here. We all know how to keep our traps shut in Crook's Hollow, don't we... You don't give me that envelope? Clyne here gets a new smile.'

Thor could read the top line of the document. TR1: Land Registry Transfer of Title. There were boxes to fill in underneath, and they were all completed – even the box at the bottom that contained Thor's forged signature. It was a good one, and he knew why. When they were kids, Rue had taught him how to do it. The desire for the deeds was explained. With both this form and the deed itself? The land could swap hands without bloodshed.

'You kill Clyne there'll be no deal,' Thor said.

'Of course, there will. Poor Clyne here dies in the tragic flood that hit Crook's Hollow, the very community he was trying to improve. COMUDEV sweep in the finish what he started, create a sweet little legacy for him. Sound nice, Clyne?'

Clyne said nothing, and the room fell silent. Thor pulled out the envelope, just as the front door swung open.

'Anyone home? I saw the lights on, and couldn't believe my—oh

shit.'

Jason Dwyer was wearing the same sodden overalls as the last time Thor had seen him, and his appearance was just the diversion Barry needed. Shoving Clyne aside, he dived at Thor and snatched the envelope. Thor fought back with a swinging right, forgetting his wrist was broken, but the scythe arced neatly back at him, slicing his coat right through to the flesh of his forearm.

Thor leapt back instinctively, but that was all the time Barry needed to run for the back door. It was Jason who gave chase, spraying water through the bar with a couple of leggy strides, but Thor called him off.

'Jase, leave him.'

They waited until they heard Barry leave through the rear of the pub.

'Martin, call the police and get an ambulance here for Lionel.' Martin quickly pulled himself together.

'What the bloody hell was that all about?' asked Jason, coming to Thor.

'Remember when I accused you of trying to kill me? Well, turns out I should have been accusing that guy. I'm sorry mate. I was angry, and I got it wrong.'

Thor helped Clyne up. He was cradling his face and moaning softly.

'It's alright, pal,' Jason said. 'I'm sorry I sprayed all that shitty water over you.'

'Least I deserved. Did you get here in that wagon?'

'No... Mum and Dad left earlier, same as most of the neighbours. I said I'd follow later, but the house is a mess. I was trying to find something to seal up the doors, and I came across Dad's old dinghy and motor in the garage, so I came in that. I was cruising about in it just now when I saw the lights on in the pub.'

Thor thought quickly. 'Can you take me somewhere in it?' 'It's a blast, of course I can.'

'Lionel, wait for help here. I'm sorry for the trouble, and if it's up to me, I won't be selling any land anytime soon.'

'Fuck's sake,' muttered Clyne as he sat down in the booth, pulling a silk handkerchief from his jacket pocket and dabbing his nose with it. 'Tell the police whatever you want,' Thor said, before walking out of the front door followed by Jason.

Sure enough, tied to a lamppost in two feet of water was a battered plastic dinghy, six feet long with a faded sky-blue hull and a small boxy motor rear mounted. Thor couldn't quite believe his luck.

He directed Jason against the flow, upstream on Main Street, then up a side street again where the water flowed down into the village. The rain was taking a slight break and had petered down to a keen drizzle. The village seemed to Thor to be in another dimension where the familiar streets were a canal system. This felt in no way like good old Crook's Hollow.

The motor was less of a powerhouse and more of a trier, and progress was steady but slow against the flow. Their main problem was debris, which was varied and swift as it barreled towards them on the narrow roads. Twice Thor thought they were going to be tipped overboard, once by a tree and the other by a dead cow.

The two men couldn't talk on the journey, due to the guttural rattle of the boat engine, and it gave Thor pause for the kind of reflection he wished he didn't have time for, namely that Roisin was being held captive by a man who had recently murdered someone.

Ward had obviously snapped after the death of his twin—if he was even dead; Thor had only seen a mortal-looking wound—and was looking for revenge on Thor, the man whose actions had caused it. In reality, it was their abducting Roisin that had caused Thor to go back there, and in turn made his family follow. They only had themselves to blame.

And then a new realisation hit Thor between the eyes.

Of course. And now he knew why the Crooks had kidnapped Roisin.

They were in on it together. Ward, Wendell, Tilly, and Mason. All of them, together with Rue and Barry. They knew about the land deal before anybody else, and they knew of Thor's importance to it. That's why they needed him dead.

Bastards, Thor thought. Every last one of them. He didn't have a clue how he was going to make them pay, but he knew that somehow, if he ever wanted to make peace with all the recent horrors, he'd have to.

44

Jason did a fairly admirable job of guiding the boat through the trees at the bottom of the Hollow, which had taken on the guise of a weird- looking mangrove swamp. It was only when the trees thinned out that the flow got too fast and Thor had to get out. Jason got as close to the bank as he could before Thor sat on the gunwale like a diver about to tip backwards.

'Tell whoever you can to get up here,' he said. 'And tell DCI Okpara it was Rue, Barry, and the Crooks. He'll know what that all means.'

Jason looked unsure. 'This doesn't look like the safest thing to do, Thor. You sure about it?'

'We are long past the point where I have a choice, mate.'

Jason had to gun the throttle hard just to keep the dinghy in the same spot. 'Well, here you go, pal. Go get 'em.'

Jason gave the engine a bigger rev, Thor took a breath, held it, and dove into the icy, swift flow, arms over his head. He dog-paddled for a couple of yards before managing to grab the sloped bank of the Hollow, but all he could feel was mud. He used whatever purchase he could get to pull himself along to a bush that was half submerged, then gripped it and dragged himself out.

As he started the climb up the valley wall, which was now half the height it should have been, he couldn't get over how deep the water was now. He hadn't been able to touch the bottom, and he was about six feet tall. All this water, all rushing downhill to the village. Was this the end of Crook's Hollow? At this rate, by morning nothing would be left.

The caravan loomed in the drizzle, with one light on in the living room. Would Ward really kill Roisin? Where that man was concerned, nothing was off the table. He braced himself for the worst.

As he got closer he could see that water was trickling through the gaps of the drystone wall below the caravan, and sure enough, as he looked over the wall, yet more water had pooled in Roisin's yard, coming from down at Crook's Farm. The farm stood black and dead in the distance, an abandoned husk.

Thor didn't think that the caravan was the best place to be for any of them, in its precarious position overlooking the flooded hollow and its foundations getting steadily waterlogged. But what choice did Thor have?

He rounded the caravan, and knocked, shouting: 'Ward, it's me.

You wanted me—now I'm here.'

There was no answer. Fearing the worst—that he'd been called here just to find Roisin's body in a last act of revenge—he pulled the door open.

And his world fell apart.

45

There, on the sofa, shrouded in soft candlelight, sat Rue and Roisin, having a cup of tea. Thor couldn't compute what he was seeing, so frayed were his emotions, so bruised and aching was his mind.

'Glad you made it,' said Rue. 'I bet you have some questions.'

Thor looked at Rue, but he no longer saw his sister. He didn't know quite what it was he saw, but it was not the woman he was devoted to. She didn't look smug, exactly, it was more of a steady, school-teacherly calm. As if she knew that a confrontation was expected, and was ready for it.

'Come and sit down,' she said, as she patted the sofa next to her. 'You can have some tea if you like.'

Thor was lost for words, and even if he hadn't been, he didn't know if he could speak. His life had been built on his relationship with this woman, and now it was crumbling, eroding and falling away like the outside world giving way to the rain.

He wanted to believe that she had an explanation, a rational, reasonable explanation for what had been going on, but he knew in his heart that there wasn't one.

And Roisin. What on earth was this?

'I don't want to believe this is happening. I'm not sure I know what's happening,' said Thor, as he edged inside. 'Where's Ward?'

'They're all gone,' Roisin said in a low voice. She was looking at the floor, the window, anywhere but at Thor.

'But you said he was here. You said he was holding you captive. You lied…'

'I know,' said Roisin. She looked sad, brittle, and young. She looked like a naughty little girl who had been caught red-handed and hadn't thought the consequences through.

'I'm going to get out of here, and the police can sort all this out. I know I can't anymore.' Thor started toward the door.

'No, you're not. You know we can't finish like that,' said Rue. She patted the sofa again.

Thor hoped that Jase was sending for the police like he asked him to, and if that was the case, perhaps stalling now was the best chance he could get at justice.

'Why, Rue—why?' he said.

Rue looked as if a fragment of regret might be about to show itself, but she quickly brushed it away. She smoothed her jeans and sighed.

'Do you know how hard it is, Thor? I mean, do you really, honestly know?'

'How hard what is? Being honest? Quite hard, it seems.'

'Raising four kids. Four kids on a farm, with a husband who got sacked. No income. No future except on handouts.'

'When did Barry lose his job?'

'Three weeks ago. Neither of us have slept since. Then there was this amazing opportunity.'

'An opportunity that wasn't yours to take.'

Rue's face darkened. 'You don't get to lecture any of us about taking opportunities. You let us all down when you left that field to fallow. Turned your back on every one of us.'

'"You should have got on with it." That message was from you, wasn't it?'

Rue simply raised her eyebrows and pursed her lips.

'You should have,' she said. 'If you had, then it would never have come to this.'

'The field, the car at the church, the hanging. Rue—all you and Barry?'

Rue shook her head impatiently.

'You don't understand the stress we were under! You don't know what it's been like. Things were tight when Barry had his job, never mind without it. And you, you ungrateful little shit, were sitting on more than a million quid you didn't even deserve.'

'Rue. You were the one person I relied upon, and you tried to kill me.'

She shook her head.

'It was Barry, of course, doing all that. But you'll do anything when your family's welfare is at stake. Anything. And you'd turned your back on all of us.'

'You can't lecture me on family values—you were going to sell my land under our family's noses.'

'What's a few acres in the grand scheme of things? They would have gotten over it when we explained it to them.'

'The whole point of the land gift was that we were to give it back.

That's why we fell out in the first place!'

'Mum and Dad would have listened to me! They would have. They would have understood.'

'Jesus,' Thor said, running his hands across his scalp.

Where were the police?

'How do you know her?' he pointed at Roisin, whose cuts still hadn't yet been attended to. She'd clearly never even made it into the police station.

Rue looked over at Roisin, who got up and moved to the kitchen.

She refilled her mug at the kettle, refusing to look at either of them. 'She came to me,' Rue said.

Roisin came back and took a seat next to Rue, holding her mug close to her chest, slumped forward dejectedly, stirring her tea gently with the other.

'What the fuck?' Thor said. 'She what?'

'She came to me and told me about the development—'

Rue was silenced by Roisin thrusting a knife into her throat—a paring knife she drew straight from her teacup. It wasn't a spoon she'd put in her tea.

Roisin held the blade in Rue's neck, right down to the plastic handle. Rue gargled blood, twisting to look at Roisin with unseeing, uncomprehending eyes. Thor stood paralysed with shock, unable to move.

Roisin's eyes were wide and wild as she held the knife firmly in Rue's neck. Rue flailed spastically, feebly, as blood from her severed jugular splashed in a red gush down her front and over the battered fabric of the sofa. Finally, she fell, and the blood spurted up out of her neck onto the picture window above the sofa.

Roisin pulled the knife out, and Rue lay still. Only her chest moved a little as she struggled to breathe.

Thor was still too shocked to move or to say anything. His beloved sister, who had spent the last few days trying to kill him, lay dying in front of him. It was all too much.

Part of him wanted to rush to her and see if she could be saved, but deep inside something made him hesitate, something in him appreciated the karmic qualities of the moment. That and, if the amount of blood that was spilled was anything to go by, any chance of saving her was long since departed.

'Just don't move, Thor,' said Roisin. 'I know this is unpleasant but it'll be over soon. I'm sorry about that. That's not how I wanted it to go.'

She was still brittle yet very much connected to the moment. After all the harm he had seen happen to her in the last few days, she seemed more switched on now than at any other point.

'A Crook and a Loxley,' she said, as if speaking to herself. 'It was always going to end badly.'

Thor said nothing.

'But your bastard father started all of this. Everything that has happened, started because of him. Oh—looks like she's gone now.'

Rue had stopped moving, her eyes were fixed on the ceiling, their pupils dilating. Thor shuddered at the sight, but also at the cold assessment in Roisin's voice.

'Why? Why join with Rue to betray me?' Thor said in a cracking voice.

'Why? Gosh, it's such a good question. It started out so innocently.

Everything started with the best intentions.' 'Tell me why?'

'I fell for you, very normally at first. I knew I shouldn't have, because of who you were, but I did. I had grown fascinated by you over all these years, in a sort of "the grass is always greener" kind of way. You had everything I wanted, everything I felt I deserved. I suppose the real question is, how much do you really know about me? I'm guessing from the way you've changed over the course of tonight, the answer would be quite a lot now.'

'I know. I know about it all,' Thor said grimly.

'So you know how hard it was. How bloody hard the whole thing was, all because your fucking Dad couldn't help himself. I wonder what it was—the naughtiness of it, the power? You must have got off on that, too, the fact that you were a Loxley and I was a Crook.'

Thor lowered his gaze, because he knew she was right: the forbidden nature of their relationship had been exciting.

'Well, Mum was sixteen. She wasn't a grown woman like me, able to make serious choices on her own. She was a kid who was sexually abused by a much older man. An older man who shouldn't have been anywhere near her. An older man who ruined her whole life.'

Thor knew. He had worked it out earlier, in his father's office while waves of nausea washed in his stomach.

'The families covered it up, of course. It was buried deep down as far as they could stick it. Nobody wanted to admit that had happened, least of all your father. But it all came unstuck again when I was four, and Mum killed herself. She killed herself because of the shame. The shame of what had been done to her, and the shame with which her own family treated her.'

The unchanged bedroom. The girl in the picture Thor hadn't seen before. Ward and Wendell's sister—Roisin's mother.

'And then imagine the horror my mum felt when instead of your bastard dad doing the honourable thing, and helping support the baby he had dropped on them all, he had another kid. A make-up kid, six months after I was born. An eraser, to scrub out the dirty memory of what he'd done. You.'

The reality of that set of circumstances would take years to get over. Thor could easily see how such a situation would royally and irredeemably mess a person up, and Roisin's story was a real jaw-dropper. But in this case there was obviously a point of no return, a point where something had snapped and a new realm of abject darkness had opened.

'And while things were going to utter bollocks here, you were treated to all the things I never had. The love and care that I was entitled to, because I was a Loxley, and because I had every right as much as you.'

Thor knew that Roisin wasn't straight on that; his memories of his upbringing were far less rosy than she'd made them out to be. But he didn't want to interrupt now. Not while the police were so damn close. He just had to keep her talking, even if the words were painful.

'And then they gave you that piece of land and you didn't fucking want it. The piece of land that should have been given to me. You didn't want it, you ungrateful shite.'

And there it was. The reason for it all, the motivation for the deceptions, lies, and heinous betrayals of trust. Revenge. Roisin wanted revenge on Thor because he was an apology from a father who didn't want her.

'I didn't know anybody knew anything about that…' Thor muttered.

'Have you forgotten where we are, Thor? Crook's Hollow, the swirling toilet bowl of gossip and secrets. Nothing's off the table, especially not with a sister as gobby as this one.' Roisin nodded at Rue's body. 'It's surprising what you get talking about at a rec centre yoga class.'

Rue had deceived Thor so badly, too, and that was equally as painful as what Roisin had done.

'All this time,' he said. 'You knew we were brother and sister?' 'I've known since Mum died. We all knew.'

Jesus, thought Thor. They're all fucking nuts. That look Ward and Wendell gave Thor the morning they came to see Roisin and Thor at the caravan. They were getting off on the whole perverse sickness of it all. Roisin continued.

'But then, when it came down to the offer of a deal, and Mason and Tilly saw a way out from Crook's Hollow and the shameful memories, they saw it as a way to get away from me too. The shameful half-Loxley they had living down at the bottom of the farm. When they accepted Clyne's offer, they told me in no uncertain terms that I was to have none of it. Ward and Wendell would be fine, but me? There was too much Loxley blood in me, they said, and they'd be damned if any profit from Crook's Farm would go to a Loxley. And then I remembered where I could get some payment of my own—where I could get what I was owed.'

'But we were… intimate… long before this came along,' he said. 'We'd been having sex as brother and sister, oh God, for weeks before all this happened.'

Roisin attempted a smile, and looked at him. 'Strange things happen to you when you've been outcast, abused, and tormented your whole life. Your requirements are… different.'

Thor felt a strange sympathy for her, an unwanted empathy. Despite all she had done, her story was sad. The unhappy tale of a child who needed love and care but was given neither, and became a product of her own environment, her own imaginings, and her own twisted needs.

'Roisin, how did you think you were going to get away with this?' he said.

'Oh God, I don't know. Rue and that husband of hers were doing all the leg work. I was just making sure you were in the right place at the right time, playing my role and waiting for a cheque. You just kept messing it up for them, and I'm afraid they weren't the best accomplices.'

Thor looked at Rue again. Her face was talcum-powder pale. Her decision to betray Thor had ultimately cost her her life.

'And the more messed up it got,' continued Roisin, 'the more we had to create this war between the two families to keep things going, keep putting you in harm's way and distract you from it. The bottom line was, you had to end up dead. It didn't matter how it happened. I just had to keep getting you to the right spot for it to happen, and keeping my innocence obvious.' 'So your kidnap. All staged?'

'When you'd fled the police and were on your way over, you've no idea how hard it was to run up those stairs without anybody seeing me, tie myself to that radiator, bash myself up and piss myself. If you'd bothered to check, you'd have noticed it was still warm.'

'I can't believe how stupid I've been,' said Thor, bowing his head. 'In truth, neither could we.'

Headlights swung beyond the glass. No sirens, just the swish of water.

'It's funny,' Roisin said, with abstract wistfulness, 'I'd sort of been looking forward to the end.'

The car stopped and the engine died. They heard footsteps slosh their way closer, and the door was booted open. A voice boomed in with the night.

'Have you seen this? She's his fucking sister!'

Barry Turner bellowed in disgust as he entered, holding Thor's envelope out in front of him, but he was rooted to the spot by the scene that lay before him. Thor, Roisin, his wife dead in a torrent of blood. He let out a guttural cry, long and painful, his voice shredded by the end of it.

Roisin simply sat next to the body, curling her knees up to her chest. She still looked vulnerable, almost innocent, but Thor knew nothing could be further from the truth. Darkness lurked in the strangest places, not least in the people in this room.

Barry went to Rue's side and tried to mop the blood off her with abject futility, as if he could somehow funnel it back into the wound in her neck. He got frustrated as the blood kept leaking through his fingers, making more of a sticky mess. His breathing become more ragged and frantic, and he started to howl again, like a wolf.

But he was cut short by Roisin suddenly plunging the knife into

his neck.

Barry threw himself at Roisin, who tumbled back into the back corner of the caravan as she struggled to keep the knife in place. For the caravan, the sudden shift in weight had a dramatic effect, and began to lean slowly towards the corner in which Barry and Roisin had fallen. They all froze, Barry hunched over Roisin somehow still with a knife in his neck.

The caravan teetered back, not quite making it level. Thor heard a couple of loud crunches outside, which jolted the flimsy shell of the caravan.

The drystone wall below the back corner, on which the van was half-perched…

The flow of water had all been too much. With a sickening tilt, the caravan began to roll back towards Roisin and Barry as the wall outside finally gave way. Thor was thrown towards the kitchenette as the world began to tumble, the lone candle flying off the table, spraying hot pink wax. Everything went black, and Thor's body was battered from top to bottom as he bounced from this to that surface, before their fall was abruptly slowed by a huge crash and the rush of freezing water.

The caravan had fallen from the valley wall right down into the flowing flood of the Hollow. Thor could just about make out the roof (or was it the floor?) bending like a cardboard box as water flushed in through the front door. He couldn't see Roisin or Barry; couldn't see anything clearly.

He crawled to the front door and shut it in an attempt to stop the caravan from sinking, but water was spraying in icy fountains from cracks in the window frames.

For now, the caravan was just about afloat, but Thor could feel its movement. The flow had them, and was funneling them downstream at a quickening pace.

Suddenly, the struggle started up again in what remained of the living room. Thumping and scrabbling. Thor couldn't get his bearings to get to them, nor did he know what he would do if he could. The sounds of struggle seemed to slow, and Barry hissed the word bitch with bile-flecked venom.

Then another impact rocked them, a scraping, shunting, sideways impact. The caravan had started to pinball through the trees at the bottom of the hollow, picking up speed and cannoning this way and that. Thor couldn't even try to stay upright, so he curled up on the floor, covered his head, and hoped it would please, please, for God's sake end.

And somewhere out there, beyond the swell, sirens started wailing.

46

As Thor later found out, the police arrived just in time to see the caravan disappear over the edge of the Hollow, and eventually lost sight of it as it clattered through the first rank of trees.

At some point, Thor had taken a heavy knock—in a series of them. He couldn't remember any of what had happened until he was awoken by the intrusive light of a paramedic's torch as the man checked his pupils. He was still in the caravan, and it was daylight. And when they eventually pulled him from the wreckage of the caravan, he saw that its roof was missing, and that it had come to rest on its side in the primary school playground, right in the centre of Crook's Hollow, and he was being rescued by a team in boats.

He remembered seeing Jason, vaguely recalled high-fiving him weakly while flat on a stretcher, and he remembered DCI Okpara overseeing the scene from the bow of one of the boats, like an admiral in a three-piece suit.

In hospital, in a private room this time, he went over everything with Okpara. He held nothing back, told him everything, starting with the envelope his father had left him. His dad's one last attempt at explaining himself, at coming clean and trying to make amends. The deeds to his property, the fake will created by Rue and Barry... and Roisin's birth certificate, proving beyond doubt her parents were Wilkes Loxley Sr. and Millicent Crook, the lost daughter of the Crooks. He told him what Rue and Roisin had told him, that they had concocted a plot to kill him out of desperation and revenge—and for money.

Okpara in turn told him that Barry and Rue's bodies had been recovered, each with near identical neck wounds that corroborated Thor's story. The envelope was nowhere to be found, just like Roisin, who, dead or alive, was still missing, but Crook's Hollow was still mostly underwater. The village was in shambles, and would take time to heal and settle. Just like Thor.

A few days later, Okpara came back with more news. The Crooks had been stopped trying to get their trailer onto a ferry into Europe, and after a few days of questioning, using evidence gathered from Crook's Farm, they eventually buckled and confessed to Ward's murder of Wilkes Sr., the circumstances surrounding Millicent's apparent suicide at twenty, and the subsequent systematic abuse of Roisin, who had become a living symbol of everything they despised.

Thor hated what Roisin had done to him, and was completely repulsed by it, but he nevertheless felt an uneasy, if genuine, sympathy for her. She was his sister, after all, a fact that he was slowly coming to terms with.

Thor also got word that the local council had come to their senses. After the natural disaster that had occurred in Crook's Hollow, no development plans would be approved in the area for the foreseeable future. All deals were off. Clyne and COMUDEV had slunk away.

As things got back to normal, and the waters of Crook's Hollow gradually receded, things began to make sense to Thor: the 'runt' of the litter, the afterthought. He was an apology, his very existence was a 'sorry.' No wonder he had struggled to bond with his mother—he was a living reminder to her of his father's infidelity.

And that was what he resolved to fix. He had wrongs he needed to right, and his mother was where he wanted to start.

And that's what he was now doing. Three weeks after the night that saw her husband murdered, Thor was sitting with his mother, Bunny, in her small living room at the council-provided retirement community in Windle Heath.

She was inundated with visitors since moving in, her children and their children. The loss of Rue and Wilkes Sr. was a sore blow to them

all, and while the family would remain shell-shocked for some time, the crimes that had been revealed muddied the extent of their grief, rendering it unclear. Like Crook's Hollow, life for them would never be the same again. But life had to go on some way.

'I don't know how you stayed with him, Mum,' said Thor, as he brought his mother a cup of tea through from the kitchen into the living room. Christmas was coming, but that didn't stop a little winter sun splashing through the bay window by Bunny Loxley's chair. The tea sloshed in the china cup, one of the few things salvaged from the shambles of Loxley Farm.

'Love makes you do funny things,' she replied. The profound simplicity of the statement took Thor aback. He had been so dismissive, so wrong. So blind to the strengths of his mother, who had done anything she could to keep her family together. Yes, she hadn't been perfect, but she had tried. He owed her that same effort.

'My brothers and sisters OK?' he asked after a moment. He knew they had rented a house together on the outskirts of the village, seemingly unable to break tradition just yet. Rue's children were with them, swallowed up by love and concern and routine, as were Wilkes Jr.'s. Thor thought it sounded rather happy, but he couldn't bring himself to join them. He was his own man, and always had been.

'Yes, they are, by all accounts. Mercy is looking after Rue's children. It'll take time, but I think the end of the farm will be good for them.' She glanced around the room, taking it in, and her eyes settled out of the window. 'This change will be good for us all, in the end. Living life in a bubble can blind you to all sorts.'

The doorbell rang and Thor got up and answered it. It was DCI Okpara. He held out his hand to shake Thor's but on seeing the plaster cast on Thor's right wrist and hand, quickly dropped it.

'Forgive the intrusion. I thought you'd be here,' he said. 'It's OK. Do you need to come in?'

'No, just a quick word with yourself is all I'm after.' 'Go for it.'

'First, I wanted to apologise to you again for not getting to the bottom of things sooner—'

Thor interrupted him. 'You don't need to say that again. Nobody could have seen where it would end up. You were doing your job, and anyone would have done the same.'

Okpara nodded slightly in thanks. 'Be that as it may, my authority would have been better placed following your lead.'

'You're a good bloke, Okpara. Don't worry about it.' Okpara smiled, but the smile quickly faded.

'There's more… The flood water has all but receded, and… we found her. Roisin Crook.'

Thor didn't know how to react to this news.

'Her body was found stuck in the roots of a leylandii hedge at one of the more well-to-do properties on the southern side of the village.'

After a moment, Thor said: 'Thank you for letting me know.'

The sun threatened to push through high above them, but the stubborn winter clouds were holding firm. Okpara made no move to leave, but stood looking at Thor.

'What happened to you was terrible, Thor. But what happened to her was very bad too, what her family, what those twin uncles of hers did to her… She would have gone to jail for a very long time for her crimes. But nobody should have gone through what she did.'

'I understand.'

Okpara patted his sides. there was nothing else for him to say. Now Roisin had been found, everything would be turned over to the Crown Prosecution Services. It was their problem now.

'Take care of yourself,' Okpara said. 'See you round.'

Thor shut the door and leaned against it. He held himself still and had a silent moment for his sister, who had suffered so much—and had done terrible things. But Okpara was more than right: none of it should have happened. He tried to ignore the repulsive reality of what happened and the grim sordid history that had made her who she was.

Thor tried to imagine an alternate universe where he had a sister who was a similar age to him, who he had grown up happily with, in the right way. He didn't know whether he would ever get comfortable with the thought of thinking of Roisin as his sister, but like everything else, he would try. And he was a trier—he knew that much.

He went back through to his Mum.

END

Acknowledgements

All my gratitude to the following:

Thank you to everyone at Endeavour Media, who I simply love working with - James Faktor, Rebecca Souster, Rufus Cuthbert, Alice Rees, Imogen Streater, Hannah Groves, Amy Burgwin, Sophy and Matthew Lynn - You are all brilliant!

Thank you to Reagan Rothe, David King, and Justin Weeks.

Thanks to Ted Gilley for his excellent editorial work on the book, that really set it on the right path.

To early readers: Mum, Dad, Tom Pickup and James Stuart. Your thoughts and feedback were always invaluable and kept the show on the road.

To Danielle Ramsay, Steph Post, Torquil MacLeod, David Joy, and Adrian McKinty - for being constant inspirations, and for reading this book and lending your words.

To Linda MacFadyen, for always putting me and my books in the right place at the right time.

To Linda Langton. Eternal thanks to yourself and everyone at Langtons International Agency.

To my wife Becky, and my amazing children Avalyn, Sylvia and Robin. No words get close. Love you all.

To Mum and Dad, Jonny, Susie, Charlotte and Abigail, and Lauren, Matt and Max - love you all and thank you for always supporting me. What a family…

To all my friends and family. Thank you for pushing me on and always having my back.

And simply - to every reader. Thank you.

Printed in Great Britain
by Amazon